REVENGE OF THE NYMPH

THE FAIRIES: VOLUME II

RAMÓN TERRELL

TAL PUBLISHING

ONE

Fecanya swung her legs back and forth, magic sparkles trailing her ankles. She leaned back on her hands and let her head fall back. From her perch on the second story windowsill, she could see the late-night clouds drifting past the moon. An owl glided overhead and landed on a nearby branch. It swiveled its head in her direction and she could have sworn its beak was clamped shut to keep from laughing.

She adjusted her brown burlap dress and nearly elbowed the sack next to her off the sill. She hurriedly snatched it off the edge and pressed it against the window with a relieved sigh. Just the thought of gathering up scattered teeth all over the street below was enough to make her shudder.

Fecanya leaned to the side and looked in the window—again—at the parents sitting on their little daughter's bed. She sighed and let her head fall against the side of the house with a thump. What was it with little humans and not wanting to sleep? Or stay still? Or not eat even when hungry? Or ...

She gave her head a shake and sighed again, resting her hand on the sack of teeth beside her. How in Lilith's underworld did humans think their young could fall asleep in a room bursting with stimuli?

Against the closest wall sat dolls atop a toy box. Portraits of cartoon characters, heads and eyes far too large to be anatomically correct, adorned each of the four fuchsia walls, and pink drapes hung drawn away from the window Fecanya sat next to. A dollhouse sat next to a little tea table for said dolls, and a three-foot-tall castle sat against the far wall where Jack Vorgamish and his Mighty Morgander Men action figures stood guard.

"Patience," she told herself. I'm not processing crap, after all." Once again she leaned to the side to look in the window, wondering if things would cross into the one hour mark as the parents struggled mightily to get their daughter to sleep.

"Hush, little baby, close your eyes. Lie in the bed, it's sleepy time. Place your tooth under your pillow ... under your pillow ... um ...your pilloooow ..."

Sucking on her thumb, little Tyleshia's blank stare turned into a confused frown as she watched Mama's mouth bob open and closed. She was far too young to know that Mama was, in fact, fishing through the depths of her vocabulary for a word that rhymed with "pillow" like a fisherman trawling a puddle for a sturgeon.

Tyleshia giggled. "You're funny, Mama. You look just like a fishie." She made popping sounds as she bobbed her mouth open and closed.

"... It'll fall away like the leaves of a Weeping Wiiiilllooooow ..."

Beside Mama, Daddy's brow crinkled. He folded his lips under his teeth as he gently patted Mama's shoulder. "Time for bed now, little lady."

Tyleshia smiled, rubbing her little tongue over the smooth exposed gums where two of her teeth had once resided. "When will she come, Daddy?"

"Well," Daddy said. "The tooth fairy only comes when you sleep, so you'd better ..."

"Do you think she'll bwing something coowl, like a hamma?"

Mama and Daddy shared a look. "A ... hammer?" Mama asked.

Tyleshia nodded, still sucking on her increasingly soggy thumb. "You think she'll bwing me a hamma, like Thowa?"

Mama's mouth formed a crinkled line to match daddy's brow. "Um ... honey, the tooth fairy doesn't trade hammers for teeth ..." She then frowned and tilted her head to the side. She looked at Daddy, then looked around the room. "Did you hear that?"

"Hear what?" Daddy asked, following her gaze to everywhere.

Mama glanced at the window. "It sounded ... it sounded like someone sighing. Like a high-pitched, *very* impatient sigh. You didn't hear it?"

Daddy shook his head. "I didn't hear anything ..."

A child's mind can either move from subject to subject with the dexterity of a squirrel, or lock onto a single topic with the strength of an angry lobster's grip. Little Tyleshia's mind went down the second option.

"You don't think the toofairy will bwing me a hamma like Thowa?"

"Er ... that's a rather unconventional thing—"

"What's unconneshinal?"

Daddy scratched his head. "Unconventional means—"

"Thowa is uh Assguardian, isn't he?"

Mama's eyes widened. "Say what?"

Daddy cupped his fist over his mouth and coughed.

"I don't think—" Mama stuttered.

"I wanna be uh Assgardian like Thowa."

"Honey, it's pronounced—"

"If the toofairy won't bwing me a hamma, how can I be uh Assgardian?"

Daddy patted Tyleshia's leg. "Honey, it's time to go to sleep. We'll talk about Azzzzzguardians, hammers, and such, later. Okay?" He offered her a thumb's up.

Tyleshia nodded, withdrew her thumb from her mouth with a 'pop', and held it up.

"Oh, good grief."

"There it is again!" Mama said. She looked around the room, then at Daddy. "Did you hear it that time?" She knelt and looked under the bed, then skulked around the room. She opened the Morgander Men castle and peeked inside. The purple-haired Raggedy Dan and Mandy dolls hanging on the closet swing back and forth when Mama opened the door to look inside. "You heard that, right? A little munchkin voice?"

Daddy yawned. "Probably one of the neighborhood kids or something." He gently grabbed Mama's shoulders and guided her toward the door.

Little Tyleshia watched them exit, though she, too, had heard the voice.

So snugly settled within the comfort of the early sunrise of her life, little Tyleshia hadn't yet acquired the concept of tired. She couldn't know, for instance, that although Daddy had *also* heard the little exasperated voice, he was, in fact, exhausted.

Tyleshia giggled in her lack of the concept of desperation, also. She didn't really know what work was, but Mama and Daddy spoke often about it, in addition to Tyleshia's endless well of energy for play, games, and a masterful skill for destruction of none but the most valuable of objects.

She twiddled her thumbs in complete obliviousness of Daddy's desperation for Tyleshia to fall asleep, rather than her becoming fully alert over a strange voice, no matter what it was.

Tyleshia giggled again when she heard the disembodied voice grumble, "who're you calling a munchkin, sister?" She replaced her thumb to her mouth and resumed syphoning out the remaining moisture. "Who's theya? Are you my toofairy?"

A much louder sigh answered, followed by a muttered, "Here we go". A throat cleared. "I ... I am *indeed* the fairy you speak, come to collect your newly fallen teeth."

Tyleshia managed to sag at this news despite lying flat on her back. "Oh. I was hoping you was the toofairy. I wanted the toofairy to come."

"WHAT DO YOU THINK I JUST ... ahem. I am *indeed* the tooth fairy, little tyke. Come to collect your *teeth* this night."

Tyleshia smiled around her thumb. "Did you bwing me a hamma?"

After a rather lengthy pause, the voice answered, "Although I have no hammer for you, for your lovely teeth I have a dime or two. Let me fish within my purse, some lovely coins—"

"If you don't have a hamma, can I have a Bwick Cwaft Builduhs kit?"

From the corner of her eye, Tyleshia saw a flicker of sparkles near the window.

"A freaking *what?*" Another sparkle burst. "Ahem. While I don't have—"

"What about a magic bubble bag?" Tyleshia negotiated.

" ..."

Tyleshia looked around the dark room during the prolonged silence. "Are you theya, toofairy?"

The resulting slow, deep breath was closer than the window, this time. Tyleshia sat up and looked in the direction of the sound, but nothing was there. She climbed out of bed and walked toward the sound. "Where are you, toofairy?" She opened the Morgander Men castle, but found only more intricately posed Morgander Men.

Staring at the action figures, Tyleshia began to imagine mighty Jack Vorgamish summoning a battle morgander into battle.

The voice of the invisible fairy drew her out of her rapidly constructing scenario.

"I ... your requests have given me pause, for you have mistaken me for Santa Claus."

Tyleshia's little brown eyes twinkled. "I wuv Sanna Caws."

"Look, kid! Can we focus? I've got a lot more of these damned dimes ... ahem. Although I'd *love* to chat all night, many more teeth I must collect, little tyke."

"Can I see you, Miss Toofairy?"

"Nope."

Tyleshia looked back to her pillow, where she heard muffled versions of the same funny words Mama and Daddy used when their feet happened upon one of her stray Brick Craft Builder's Bricks.

She hopped back in bed and lifted the pillow, but her tooth was gone, and no fairy. She dropped her head on the pillow, then giggled again when she heard more grumbling.

"Oof. You trying to crush me? How does Tootheria get these things out from under these huge heads?"

When the bumping finally stopped, Tyleshia waited silently in the dark room, her little night light valiantly battling the darkness. "Are you weaving now, Miss Toofairy?"

"Indeed I am, lovely girl. I must depart with a twirl!"

"Why you gonna twirl?" Tyleshia asked, gnawing on her thumb.

"Dunno. Rhymes with girl."

"What's whymes?"

"The time has come for me to leave. And you, beautiful girl, time for sleep."

Tyleshia turned over and fished her little hand under her pillow again. This time, her little fingers closed around a large silver coin. She drew her hand out and grinned. She turned back to the empty space the voice occupied.

"It's a lot bigger than the last one you bwought. Thank you, Miss Toofairy." She offered a wide smile to the room, otherwise dark except for the ambient glow of the two competing nightlights at the opposing walls. "I wuv you, Miss Toofairy!"

She heard the faint sound of "Aww, you're so sweet," followed quickly by a loud clearing of a throat and a more audible, "you're ... welcome sweet child, and thanks for the teeth! May you have dreams that are ever so sweet!"

After several moments of silence followed, Tyleshia heard the faintest of sighs. It sounded like the same sigh Mama and Daddy made when Tyleshia followed them into the bathroom with her toys.

Suddenly the room lit in a burst of sparkles. Brilliant golden light shined on the tooth fairy's light brown dress, which looked to Tyleshia to be made of the same material as the sack Daddy brought potatoes home in.

The tooth fairy floated in the golden light, wings fluttering behind her arched back. Her teeth gleamed in a broad—yet somehow pained—smile across her glowing face.

Little Tyleshia giggled and put her coin down to clap. The tooth fairy zipped out of the window in a trail of sparkles, and Tyleshia grabbed her coin and trotted out the door to show a soon to be very surprised—or rather, unnerved—Mama and Daddy her silver dollar.

Two

Teeth.

Fecanya glided through the many snaking tunnels on her way to the Arizona branch of Fey World Maintenance Services. As much as she tried not to admit it to herself, that first little girl had been cute. Of all the children she'd visited, tonight, the first girl had also had the least greasy teeth. What did children do with their mouths to make their teeth so greasy?

She banked a left turn and sped down a winding tunnel, passing a swarm of brownies who'd merged to become a broom to sweep out the dust and grime. They briefly reconfigured to form a hand and waved at the Ordure Engineer-turned Temporary Tooth Fairy.

Fecanya waved at the brownies as she passed. She zipped down another tunnel where a team of dwarves hacked at a precious mineral deposit with pickaxes. They struck to the rhythm of cadences chanted by dwarves who'd managed to convince everyone that chanting cadences was just as labor-intensive as the actual labor. Singing was all in the diaphragm, you see.

Up, she flew, ascending yet another winding tunnel that eventually arced vertical again. A pinprick of light shone in the distance and rapidly grew more prominent as Fecanya raced toward it. The distant sounds of the busy rotunda sharpened as she neared the end of the tunnel.

Fecanya burst free of the tunnel in a dramatic flourish, zinging ever upwards in the middle of the grand rotunda. Beehive-style living pods passed in a blur as she flew straight up toward the upper levels. Far below, she heard Davin Gravelchin's rumbling voice.

"Well, look who's got a buncha sparkle in her wings!"

Fecanya looked down at the waving dwarf and smiled.

She swung herself over the rail of the appropriate pathway and skipped along toward her appointment with the resident therapist. Children's teeth might be a touch of disgusting at times, but they were still better than the other ... merchandise she usually worked with.

The Ordure Engineer-turned substitute Tooth Fairy—stopped outside the door to Leowitriss's office and snapped her fingers. A sweetbark cigarette appeared in a burst of purple sparkles. She grinned deviously at the little stick as if it were in on her private joke, then grimaced after placing the cigarette between her lips. The sweetbark had long ago lost its charm, as did the actual smoking of it. But the way Leowitriss's jowls trembled when he shook his head in disapproval made it worth the discomfort.

Fecanya opened the door, stepped in, closed the door, then knocked.

Spectacles balanced precariously at the tip of his nose, Leowitriss raised his ram-horned head to regard her. He opened his mouth, then simply shook his head and indicated the chaise lounge against the wall.

Fecanya skipped over and plopped down. And bounced.

"Ow!" She sat up and rubbed the back of her head and her backside. "What'd you do to this couch? Feels like a slab of cement."

"Urhem." Leowitriss slid his spectacles up the bridge of his nose and rubbed the space between his eyes.

"Still getting headaches?" Fecanya asked. "You're head's probably too big for those—"

"Given your newly developed habit of falling asleep during our sessions," Leowitriss said rather sharply. "I felt it necessary to make the *chaise lounge* a bit less comfortable."

Crinkled sweetbark cigarette dangling from the corner of her mouth, Fecanya blinked at him. "I thought these sessions were supposed to be relaxing, Leo. What's more relaxing than you droning on about 'theh responsibiliteeehs of your job, huhMiss Fecanyah!'"

"I do NOT tuck in my chin like that when I talk! He glanced down at his chin and pushed it out. "And put that cigarette out. Please!

"Sure, Leo."

"My *name*—"

"Is ... huhLeowitriss, Miss huhFecanyah!" Fecanya boomed.

Leowitriss ground his teeth, then glared at the pen he was strangling. After several deep breaths, he pulled up a chair beside her. "Why must you mock me so? I'm here to *help* you."

Fecanya considered the question. She didn't dislike the therapist, after all. What could be more endearing than a prim and proper satyr, dressed in hummus-colored, striped slacks, pale orange shirt, rose and rhubarb tie, and wingtips?

No, she didn't dislike Leowitriss at all. Perhaps it was the fact that she was forced into these sessions. Maybe it was because Leowitriss had taken it as his personal mission to "fix" her. Or, perhaps it was simply because it was just too easy to get him going.

"Well, you know what they say, Leo," Fecanya began, then quickly added, "witriss! We tease the ones we love the most." She glanced at her sweetbark cigarette, blue smoke drifting lazily toward the ceiling, and put it out. She tossed it in the air and it disappeared in a puff of blue sparks.

Leowitriss placed three sausage-like fingers over his heart and tilted his ram-horned head. "Oh, Miss Fecanya. That is so very kind. In a kind of elbow to the throat kindness, but kindness nonetheless. Thank you."

Fecanya resisted the urge to echo his breathy "huhthankyou," and just rolled with it. The starchy satyr might make a human tax collector look like a heavy metal roadie after ten energy drinks, but he was trying.

"Now," Leowitriss folded his hands in his lap. "You've been sticking to your exercise regimen as prescribed, hmm?"

Fecanya leaned back into the granite-like cushions. "Well, I've been going and doing my best. But, I'd rather not get too muscly, you know?" She held up a skinny little arm. "I don't think it'd be very fairy-like to go around with arms like a dwarf, after all. Be tough for flying."

"You needn't be concerned," Leowitriss replied, swallowing the bait with the single-mindedness of a largemouth bass. "It is rather impossible for a fairy to attain the physique of a dwarf."

"Are you sure?" Fecanya asked, her tone as innocent as a humming siren. "I mean, it'd be nice to lift five times my weight, but I'm afraid it would be rather unsightly. I mean, how do you manage it? You've got some pretty hard-looking ham hocks on you. I bet you could manage loads of weight with those things."

Leowitriss's chin wrinkled with pride as he looked over his biceps. "Well, I have been making my way to some of the boot camps we have around here, and the progress has been ..." he narrowed his eyes. "What's a ham hock?"

Fecanya waved a dismissive hand. "Oh it's just slang. Means you're just so *beefy*, Leowitriss. If you're not careful, you're gonna start attracting ..." she looked his outfit over, again, "um, others." She smiled.

Leowitriss narrowed his eyes. "You have the smile of a snapdragon, Miss Fecanya. Our session has ended."

Fecanya blinked. "But it hasn't begun."

"I'm sure you're devastated," came the reply. "Exercise and drink water. Maybe lace it with a little turmeric. Wheatgrass is good as well. And definitely consume as much Morgathra Root as possible."

"Morga ... what?" Fecanya frowned. "What was that last bit?"

"Morgathra Root," Leowitriss explained. "It's good for the brain, and is especially beneficial to those who tend to have the same personality traits as the objects of their profession."

Fecanya nodded at Leowitriss with surprised approval as she chewed on that for a moment. She glanced at the top of the satyr's head. "Does it help with rapidly retreating hairlines, too? You're losing the follicle war—"

"Get! OUT!"

Fecanya shot into the air and, with a figure-eight flourish, zipped out the door. She magically closed it behind her, and for just a moment, she felt a pang of hesitation. Maybe she should lighten up on ole Leo. She half-turned, thinking perhaps she would go in and try to wrangle up an apology. However, her hand stopped just before she started to knock when she heard chuckling on the other side of the door. She grinned. "Maybe there's hope for us both, Leo."

THREE

Portraits of athletic goblins flexing sweet pea-sized muscles lined the gravy-colored walls outside the workout studio of Zachary Von Badass. Fecanya's wings fluttered with the rapidity of a hummingbird, keeping her a few heads above the herd of milling dwarves.

"Why're ye floatin' about up there, sprite?" one of the dwarves asked. "Yer too good to stand on the ground with the rest of us?"

Fecanya looked down at the hulking speaker with the bright orange beard. "Nah. I prefer my oxygen armpit-funk-free."

The surrounding dwarves laughed. "She got ye on that one, Dorgin," one said beside him.

Dorgin snarled. "She's talkin' 'bout all 'o' ye!" He waved a thick arm to encompass the group.

"Speak fer yerself," said another.

The door to the workout studio swung open, jostling the multicolored beads hanging on the back. The dwarves milled in, followed by a couple of mumbling trolls who lumbered at the back of the crowd as it strangled itself through the door.

The studio was lined with mirrors on every wall which rapidly began to haze over under the burden of body heat from the mass of dwarves, goblins, and trolls.

Ballet barres lined three of the mirrored walls under which, three-foot-tall dumbbell racks sagged under the weight of no less than a thousand pounds of weights. A passing dwarf stopped and picked up a hundred-and-fifty-pound dumbbell. "Hmph. I like the rubber grip better," she grumbled, turning it this way and that.

"Ye gonna play with that or get to yer mat, Hilder?" one of the dwarves nearest Fecanya teased.

Fecanya watched as Hilder pointedly turned her head and regarded the other dwarf, who made a show of running his hand over his beard under her iron gaze.

"Maybe I'll put it down," Hilder finally replied. "Or maybe I'll come over there and touch ye on the chin with this dumbbell really, *really* fast." She tossed it in her hand a couple times like one would a palm-sized rock, then sat it back on the rack. The beleaguered apparatus let out an almost sentient groan.

"Don't know why yer even here," Dorgin said when Fecanya snickered. "What with them twig arms, there." He twiddled his fingers.

Fecanya arched an eyebrow. "Says the dwarf who's spent more time wielding a fork than a pickaxe?"

Dorgin joined in at the murmur of chuckling about the studio. "Yer a saucy one, eh?"

"Please don't think of sauce when you think of me, Dorgin," Fecanya said.

"Hum hem!" boomed—well, tried to boom—a voice from the front of the room.

Hands clasped behind his back, a lone goblin paced back and forth atop a raised platform at the front of the studio. "Time for play ... is OVER!"

Fecanya bit her bottom lip. After more than a month of classes, she still hadn't gotten used to this guy. From the dingy salmon-colored headband, wrinkled blue workout tights—that somehow managed to have creases in them—to his athletic toe shoes, the goblin was quite a sight.

In a voice much like a raging televangelist with vocal cords afire, Zachary Von Badass roared, "When you step into my battlefield, your only chance of survival is to turn on BEAST MODE!"

The goblin rammed a little gray fist into the radio, filling the studio with the song Eye of the Liger. He then leapt straight into the air and landed in the pushup position.

"It's time to push! It's time to GO!" His upper back bobbed up and down with each rep while his lower body rested comfortably on his three-inch-thick yoga mat. "And when it's time to get down, that's when I call on MAAAH friend. And his name is BHUUEEAST MOOOOOODE!"

"Sounds like somebody's chokin' him on the privy," Dorgin muttered, bending his arms as best he could despite his ample midsection doing most of the work. "You two'd make a good match, sprite." He turned a wide, toothy smile on Fecanya that shone like fresh butter.

"Worry about yourself," Fecanya shot back, bouncing through her pushups. "Or better yet, worry about cutting back on the pies."

"Oh ho," Dorgin replied, rocking back and forth through his pushups. "The little sprite here's gettin' all caught up in beast mode."

More chuckling.

"This, coming from the dwarf who's been caught up in 'Feast Mode'?" Fecanya countered, to roaring laughter.

"This. Is not. The time. To TALK!" Zachary Von Badass groan-shouted. "This is. The time. To WORK. This is. The time. To PUSH. This is the time to FIGHT. And the only way to win thiiiis fight is to dig DEEP, grab HOLD, and summon up BEAST MOOOOOODE!"

"Too bad beast mode doesn't iron his shorts," Fecanya whispered.

The goblin's ears flopped wildly as he wobbled up and down in his pushup-crazed frenzy, salmon headband a pink blur. "Every ... body COUNT! One. Two. Three. FO! I. Summon. BEAST. MODE!"

FOUR

F ecanya ran a hand along the side of the towel cone wrapped atop her head and winked at her reflection in the mirror. Despite being a purely magical being that didn't sweat or need to bathe, she loved the refreshing tingle of the moist air on her skin after a hot bath.

She closed her eyes and inhaled the aroma of bath salts with a pinch of fey dust that still floated in the air. She curled an arm in front of the mirror, flexed, then snorted. If there was a muscular fairy anywhere from here to Lilith's Underworld, Fecanya had only ever seen one. Deliah Harmass, AKA Lieutenant Commander Hardass.

"Bedtime," she yawned.

Fecanya dried her auburn hair and stretched, then hopped onto the bed. "Gotta hit Helkin Avenue tomorrow night," she said around yet another yawn. "Teeth. For the life of me, I don't get why in the world anyone would want to collect—"

She drifted to sleep.

Throughout history, many have fashioned themselves as master practical jokers. From the inventor of the whoopie cushion to the gentleman who that thought it would be funny to line the floor next to his sleeping room-mate's bed with mousetraps.

They were all wrong.

Master of the practical joke was, in fact, Time. And it was during Fecanya's fitful slumber that Time found the perfect opportunity to allow Fecanya to experience as much of her current nightmare as possible.

But even Time couldn't restrain horror indefinitely.

After what felt like an eternity, Fecanya jolted upright. She ran her fingers through her hair and swallowed as she scanned her pod. "Turds," she whispered. "Apes. Turd-flinging apes." She realized she was gasping and forced her breathing to slow. "So ... so many turds."

She curled her legs up and wrapped her arms around them, resting her chin on her knees. She took deep breaths, not daring to close her eyes for fear of seeing in her mind's eye the rain of gorilla turds, imps using a waste-water plant as a portal, and hearing the phantom voices of frantically laughing chimpanzees.

"It's over," she told herself. "Been over for months, now. No turd missiles, no filthy, *filthy* imps."

From the corner of her eye, Fecanya noticed several large bags slouched against the far wall. Teeth. Slimy, greasy, children's teeth. She'd even discov-ered a handful of adult teeth in there, much to her horror. She gave herself a shake. Humans were a special kind of primate.

She stretched her legs and swung them over the side of the bed, still regarding the sacks of teeth. "Why in Lilith's vast Underworld would a fairy *voluntarily* collect teeth?" Fecanya rolled her eyes at her own question, for she knew the answer.

"Don't care how relatively clean a child's teeth are," she mumbled. "No way I'm living in a pod made outta those things." Fecanya shuddered at the thought of living in a child tooth pod. Didn't Tootheria and her ilk know what the miniaturized humans put in their mouths?

Everything.

With great reluctance, Fecanya climbed out of bed and went to her desk where a glittering letter waited. She plopped down in the chair, and with a wave of her hand, a teacup and pitcher appeared in the air. While the pitcher filled the little ceramic cup, Fecanya opened the letter, then reached up and took the cup out of the air.

With each word she read, her mouth grew drier, despite the hot drink.

*Dear Fecanya, Ordure Engineer of Fey World Maintenance Services.
Your presence is required in my office post haste, the moment you open this
letter.*

—*Deliah Harmass,*
(Lead Supervisor at Fey World Maintenance Services)

Fecanya ran her tongue along the inside of her cheek. "*Deah, Fecanya,*"
she began to mock. *Oahduah Engineah—*"

More text appeared on the letter.

"*When I said your presence was required in my office, I did not mention
your rather colorful sarcasm, nor your recalcitrant attitude. Leave both
behind.*

—*Yours truly,*
Deliah Harmass
(LEAD SUPERVISOR *at Fey World Maintenance Services)*

A fresh retort nearly escaped Fecanya's mouth before she wrestled it back.
She stared at the paper, which seemed to stare right back at her; waiting.

After opening her mouth several times, Fecanya wrinkled her lips and
got up from the table. She hopped out of her little pod, high up in the
rotunda, and zipped across the open-air toward Deliah's office.

Fecanya smiled and saluted a group of waving gnomes as she glided by.
She let out a contented sigh. Though she'd never admit it to anyone else,
she enjoyed the industrious hum of FWMS. Magic buzzed in the air, pickaxes rose and fell, flowers bloomed, and from this high up, even the power
of dwarven body odor was diminished.

She touched down in front of Deliah Harmass's office door, still not
fully committed to entering yet. She and the Lead Supervisor didn't exactly
dislike each other so much as they got on like a pair of dueling rams.

Fecanya pressed her head to the door, and the sound of Bloomara's
muffled opera singer's voice filled her ears. The sound practically dragged a
snarl across her face, and Fecanya thought maybe she'd just go back home
and send in a sick note ..."

The door swung open.

Head still turned aside, Fecanya blinked, then straightened and began pulling at the nonexistent wrinkles in her burlap dress. Four sets of eyes stared at her while she wrestled her dignity into position and strutted through the door. "Uhem."

"*Uhem*," Deliah replied.

"Hi, Fecanya!" Sugressa waved.

"Umhey," Fecanya murmured.

Garbita cleared her throat. "Nice to see you, Fecanya."

Fecanya responded with a smile worthy of a great white shark.

"Thank you for joining us, Fecanya," Deliah said. "And now that we're all here, I need to discuss with you some rather concerning events." She looked at Fecanya. "You've been covering for Tootheria for the past couple of weeks, now. Well-done."

Fecanya responded to that by opening her mouth and keeping it that way.

"Apparently," Deliah continued, "Tootheria isn't the only Fey Services staff to have gone missing. Mewamina is reportedly MIA as well, and hasn't been heard from for a week. Without a proper replacement, kittens have not been properly taught to mew."

Sugressa raised her hand and Deliah nodded. "I've never met Mewamina, but I thought she did something else with kittens. I mean, wouldn't their mums and dads teach them to mew?"

Fecanya snorted. "You ever meet a cat that taught anyone anything other than how to be an a—"

"Cats do not meow to one another, Sugressa," Deliah cut in. "The whole meow front is something they've relied on us to teach them. If not for the Cat Communications Department of FWMS, adult cats would struggle to remain cute enough for humans to tolerate their rather ... intractable personalities."

Bloomara crossed her arms over her chest, her long blue locks falling over her shoulders. "What has been the result?"

"Groaning and grunting," Deliah Harmass answered with a sigh. "Veterinarians all over the region are reporting a surge in kitten-related visits due to their excessive grunts and groans. If we don't solve this problem soon, humans may well start misdiagnosing them as constipated."

Fecanya shuddered. "That ... that means they'll start prescribing ..." she couldn't even finish the sentence.

Deliah caught her meaning, however, and responded with a grim nod. "Yes. Laxatives. And there's more."

Everyone sagged where they stood. Fecanya thought she could feel her wings droop.

"Caffeinisa is also missing."

Garbita's eyes widened. "Oh dear. Oh dear, dear me."

Fecanya's heart skipped a beat. "Yeeeeeaaah. That's not good."

"To put it mildly," Deliah said. "Reports have come in that coffee shops all about the human metropolis, Seattle, are seeing a spike in coffee sales. So it can be surmised that without Caffeinisa's contributions, nonmagically enhanced coffee beans do little to keep adult humans going."

"So, what?" Fecanya asked. "They're oversleeping?"

"Oversleeping, falling asleep everywhere, growing irritable due to headaches, and generally just beating each other up." Deliah moved to the far wall of her office, where hung a whiteboard with a map of Washington. She pointed at a section of Seattle with a cluster of red dots.

"My dear!" Garbita held her hand over her heart. "Surely all of that can't be reports of fisticuffs?"

Fecanya side-eyed the Detritus Redistributor. *Fisticuffs*?

"Er, that is the case, Garbita." Deliah turned to the board. "So far, there have been only minor scuffles; humans kicking and slapping each other, throwing lukewarm coffee and teabags. That sort of thing. As you can see," she indicated the new dots that had appeared while she spoke. "The situation is currently isolated to Seattle, but it's spreading so rapidly, it could become epidemic within the week."

Fecanya whistled through her teeth. An entire human city without caffeine? "Welp!" She clapped her hands together. "I appreciate the heads-up, Deliah. I'll be sure to be extra careful to avoid all those *fisticuffs* while I'm collecting teeth—"

"The teeth can obviously wait," Deliah interrupted. "When you find our missing staff, you can assist Tootheria in cleaning up all the stray teeth that are no doubt littering the streets of Seattle right now. Our priority is finding our missing fairies. There's more to this, and we need to find out what. I have all confidence in the four of you to do just that."

Deliah Harmass clasped her hands behind her back as she turned to the whiteboard again. "You're dismissed. Be careful."

FIVE

"How is it that FWMS is stationed in Arizona when Washington has so much more vegetation?" Fecanya zipped between oak and pine trees, just behind Bloomara. She glanced over her shoulder to see Garbita and Sugressa zigzagging just behind.

"What difference does that make?" Bloomara asked.

Fecanya returned her attention ahead just in time to see a colossal oak speeding toward her. Eyes bulged, she gritted her teeth and banked a hard left, then right. She was back in formation behind the bloom fairy in less than a second.

"Careful, dear. You wouldn't want to *damage* the *trees*."

"Eow, of *course*, laydeh *trash* faireh," Fecanya drawled. "I wouldn't want to *daumage* the *trees*."

"I. Am. NOT a trash fairy!" Garbita brandished her wand as she whipped around a towering redwood. She dipped low, just above the ground, and with a magical flourish, swept up several plastic cups and a dingy cloth soiled by substances Fecanya didn't want to ponder too closely.

Garbita waved her wand around in a circle spinning the refuse in the air. Finally, she tapped her wand in the air, and the litter exploded in a shower of sparkles.

"The difference, Bloom," Fecanya answered, "is things would be easier if the home base was in the forest where normal fairies would operate."

"That's why we have magic, dear," Bloomara replied. "We can live anywhere."

"It smells so lovely out here!" Sugressa left a trail of pink glitter in her wake as she zipped about the trees, spreading her arms wide and spinning through the air. "It's so green and fresh! I just *love* it!" A cloud of glitter exploded from the sugar fairy when she threw her arms out again.

"You wanna stop that?"

The fairies came to an abrupt halt. Fecanya and the others glanced at each other, then at their surroundings.

"Yeah," the voice said again from somewhere near the ground back the way they'd come. "I can do without puffin puke all in my fur!"

"Puffin puke?" Fecanya stole a sidelong glance at Sugressa, who looked genuinely wounded. "Hey. Buddy!" She glided toward the direction of the voice. "You always rude to strangers?" When no answer came, she moved a little closer. "Hello? Did you hear me? We don't need some jackass yelling ..." she trailed off when she felt something soft envelope her right shoulder and part of her arm.

"Um ... Fecanya," Sugressa said from somewhere behind. Far behind.

"What's this on my arm?" Fecanya inquired through clenched teeth.

"It's a cat's paw," Bloomara answered. "Be still."

"That's right, Fecalanya," the voice whispered. "Be still."

"Turn loose my shoulder, feline."

"Or what?" came the amused reply.

"I'm a shit fairy, cat. Think about all the things I can do to make your life miserable."

The moment lingered as the cat presumably mulled the possibilities over. The paw retracted. Fecanya took a deep, steadying breath, and spun around. A gray striped tabby watched her from the edge of a tree branch.

The others hovered behind the cat, shifting nervous glances between the tabby and Fecanya. She plastered a calm facade on her face when she realized she was still within reach when the cat suddenly lifted its foreleg.

Bloomara, Sugressa, and Garbita snapped their wands at the ready, and Fecanya raised her hand to summon her own magic.

Tongue midway to foreleg, the cat froze. He looked over his shoulder at the other fairies, all midassault. "What's your problem?" They watched as he went about cleaning his leg. Then he lifted his leg higher and started to lick his belly.

He opened his mouth wide, revealing two long sets of needle-like teeth. Tongue hanging down his chin, he then went about the most unnatural-looking task of cleaning his chest.

"What's your spine made of?" Fecanya asked. "Gelatin?"

"Don't be jealous just because you can't do it."

"I also don't bathe in spit," Fecanya replied.

The cat shrugged and kept bathing.

"Alrighty, then." Fecanya made her way to the other fairies just as the cat sat down and lifted one of his hind legs. She looked over her shoulder at the bathing feline and shook her head. "Let's just leave him to it."

"Maybe he might know—" Sugressa began.

Garbita waved an irritated hand. "Let's just make our way to Seattle and leave that dis-*gusting* creature to his business."

A crisp breeze slithered through the forest, drifting between the trees and small foliage, rustling a bed of leaves. Somewhere overhead, a blue jay called out. After a rather embarrassing silence, it let out several more—rather indignant—calls that grew farther away.

"If all puffins'r like you lot," the cat replied to Garbita, "it's no wonder you're being taken away." He continued his task, pointed ears stabbing into the air repeatedly as his cleaned the same spot on his chest that had become quite moist at this point.

"What did you say?" Bloomara demanded. "You know about the abductions?"

"Yup."

Fecanya made a valiant effort at ignoring the water trough slurps coming from over the cat's shoulder. "Er, you mind postponing all that until we finish talking, please?"

The tabby twisted around to look at them, then licked his chops. "Hm?"

"I'll be right back." Sugressa darted around the back of a tree.

Fecanya's mouth turned down, and she bit her bottom lip at the first sounds of retching. "I said, can you tell us about some missing fairies."

"Yeah," the tabby said.

The fairies waited, Sugressa retched some more behind the tree, and the cat blinked at them.

High in the overcast sky, a gaggle of dark gray rain clouds stopped directly overhead. In typical Washington rain cloud fashion, they lingered rather threateningly.

Fecanya glanced up at the congregation that, despite being formless, she was sure smirked back at her. She waved irritably at the cat. "Well?"

"Well, what?" the cat asked innocently.

"About the missing fairies?"

"Yeah, what about them?" the tabby asked.

Fecanya altered her irritable waving into an intricate pattern. In less than a couple seconds, she could drum up a big enough wave of magic and ram a huge...

Garbita tackled her from the side, and the two tumbled head over heels through the air until righting themselves. "Not *yet*, Fecanya. We *must* get the infor*mation* first."

Fecanya glared at the tabby—sitting with his tail wrapped around his paws—and nodded.

"We'd like you to tell us what you know about the missing fairies," Bloomara explained.

"Oh, well, why didn't you say so?"

"We already did."

"No, you didn't. You just asked if I knew about it." He began cleaning his nether regions. Directly facing Bloomara. The bloom fairy closed her eyes and turned her head aside.

Next to Fecanya, Garbita pinched the bridge of her nose. "Can you *please* tell us *about* the *fairies*?"

The cat stopped midlick and looked from Garbita to Fecanya. "Why's she talk like that? She's so ..." He raised himself up to his full sitting height and began to wobble his head.

"Fffffffff!" With a dramatic flourish, Garbita yanked her wand out of thin air.

Bloomara gasped and waggled her fingers. "Fecanya! Stop her!"

Giggling, Fecanya looked past the enraged garbage fairy at the panicked Bloomara, then sighed and rushed around in front of Garbita. "Not now. Not now. Let's hear what he has to say first." She bit her bottom lip as she watched Garbita's teeth digging into her wrinkled bottom lip, nostrils flared, green bun at the top of her head wiggling with indignation.

"Out of my way, Fecanya!" Garbita tried to wave her wand over

Fecanya's shoulder. "I'll turn that ill-mannered moggie into a *rat* and drop him into a *sewer*!"

Fecanya held onto Garbita's wrist and tried not to fall over as they fumbled through the air. "As much as I'd like to see that, we need to find out what he knows. Oof!" She had to hold on when Garbita nearly tossed her aside. "You've been hitting Zachary Von Badass's boot camps?"

"Garbita! Control yourself." Bloomara's wings fluttered, and she zipped past the sniggering cat to hover beside the struggling pair. "That's an order!"

After a few moments of teeth-gnashing reluctance, Garbita relaxed, and Fecanya released her. "Fine." She crossed her arms over her chest. "Let's just get *on* with it."

Bloomara watched the detritus redistributor for a moment longer, then nodded in satisfaction before flying back to the amused tabby. "If we can dispense with the nonsense, feline?"

The cat's responding yawn again displayed a couple of healthy sets of fangs. "Are we done?"

Fecanya frowned. She looked at Bloomara, who seemed equally dumbfounded.

Rustling around a nearby tree announced a recovered Sugressa's return. Fecanya pressed her lips together. Poor girl. "You all right, there? You're looking a little green."

Sugressa's downturned mouth looked as though she'd re-tasted the last remnants of whatever she'd had for breakfast. She nodded. "M'fine. Thanks."

"We haven't begun yet, feline," Bloomara said. "We were asking about—"

"Did you see that?" The cat sat erect and looked over his shoulder.

Fecanya watched as his pointy-eared head jerked left and right as he tracked a falling leaf as it rocked back and forth in the air to settle on the ground. He hopped from branch to branch until finally landing next to the leaf.

"What in Lilith's Underworld is that fool doing?" Garbita growled.

Fecanya watched as the cat shuffled his hind legs and sat down, then began scooting the leaf around on the forest floor.

Fecanya shook her head. "This is amazing. I don't think I've ever encountered such a perfect lack of focus." He dropped on his side and rolled onto his back, scratching at the leaf. Midswing, he stopped, curled up into a sitting position, and started to lick one of his hind legs. After precisely four licks, he turned his attention back to the leaf.

Fecanya glanced at Bloomara, who took several measured breaths. "Can you please wrestle that jumble of hopping crickets of a brain of yours into focus for a few moments, feline? Please!"

The cat stopped midswat and looked up at her. "No need to get your little wings all wrinkled." He rolled over and sat up, tail wrapping around his paws again. Whatcha want?"

Bloomara's eyes widened like saucers. She opened her mouth and Fecanya thought she was about to bite the cat, with all those teeth showing. Instead, she closed her eyes and exhaled through her nose. "We'd like you to share what you know about some kidnapped fairies you said you saw, feline."

"Okay. First of all, *puffin*, mine name's not 'feline'—"

Bloomara thrust her fists down at her sides. "I. AM. NOT. A. PUFFIN!"

"Second ..." he suddenly looked at his left shoulder and started cleaning it.

Fecanya looked at Bloomara and saw her wand-hand twitch.

His shoulder sufficiently cleaned, the cat continued. "Second, my name isn't 'feline.'"

"You just clarified that," Bloomara growled.

"Careful your blood pressure, Bloomara," Sugressa warned.

"My blood pressure's fine."

The cat started to clean himself.

"Feline ..."

The cat gave her a lazy look. "My name's not 'feline'."

"Fine! Then what is your blasted name?"

"You really don't have to be so aggressive," the cat stated. "I hear puffins can be fragile in the heart territory."

Fecanya pressed her lips together so tightly they felt like they would fuse shut. *This is fantastic.*

Bloomara stared at the cat for several moments, mouth hanging open. She closed her eyes yet again and asked in a voice as soft as cotton-wrapped iron. "What might your name be?"

The cat sat up and pushed out his chest. "Diesel."

Fecanya arched an eyebrow. "Diesel. You're name's Diesel?"

Diesel answered with a curt nod.

"All right then, er, Diesel," Bloomara said around her jackal-like smile. "What, pray tell, do you know of any missing fairies?"

"I know that several times I saw a rather scantily clad woman trotting through here with a sack over her shoulder. There was some muffled cursing coming from the bag. I know puffins can talk, but you lot have some foul vernacular at your disposal."

"How do you know they were fairies?" Bloomara asked.

"I saw a few puffs of that sparkly stuff you all do," Diesel said with a shrug.

"Which way did she go?" Fecanya asked.

Diesel pointed to the south. "West. Toward the place where all the two-legged servants clump together."

"Seattle?" Fecanya said.

Diesel shrugged again. "I guess."

"Anything else?" Bloomara pressed. "Did she say anything; give any indication of what she was doing or why she kidnapped those fairies."

"Nope. But I've heard puffins is good eatin', so maybe she's doing groceries for a barbecue." He licked his chops.

Fecanya crossed her arms over her chest and rose into the air to hover over Diesel. "If you even insinuate dining on one of us," Fecanya said, "I'll fill your mouth with something barbecued that you won't like, you raggedy fur-covered bunion."

"Will you relax?" Diesel said. "You're almost as bad as that stupid flock further west. Can't *stand* those feathery bastards."

Bloomara nodded. "South to Seattle. Right. Mr. Diesel is there anything else?"

Diesel looked up from his armpit. "Hm?"

Six

"I really don't know why you're so resistant to doing your job," Bloomara said.

Fecanya resisted the urge to glare at Bloomara. Instead, she settled for rolling her eyes. "That's not my job, right now."

"You are an ordure engineer first and foremost—"

"You'll have to take that up with Deliah," Fecanya interrupted. "I'm to sub in for Tootheria until we find her."

"I bet you want *so* badly for us to *find* her," Garbita remarked.

"I'm here, aren't I, garbage girl?"

"Garbage—" Garbita took a deep breath. "You are *such* a pill, Fecanya."

Fecanya held her fingers over her heart and mouthed the words as Garbita spoke them. Then, from the corner of her eye, she saw Garbita's face go from angry pink to furious lava red.

"You have the worst attitude I've ever seen, Fecanya." Bloomara turned her perpetual disapproving stare on her. "Why must you be this way?"

"Why must you act like you're applying for the position of Assistant Lieutenant Commander Hardass?" Fecanya shot back. "And anyway," she waved a hand in Garbita's general direction. "She started it."

"You're changing the subject," Bloomara said. "Just because you are temporarily filling in for Tootheria doesn't mean you can shirk your duties as ordure engineer."

"Feel free to share the load, then," Fecanya offered. "You play with flowers, Bloom. *Flowers.*"

"It's an important job."

"Not saying it isn't. But your job entails talking to bees and fondling flowers."

"I do NOT—"

"I know you're jealous," Fecanya pushed on. "I mean, who wouldn't want to process shit while collecting children's—and sometimes adults'—*lovely* teeth part-time?"

Bloomara gasped. "Mind your language, Fecanya!"

"Yeah, right. I'm a shit fairy. Take it up with Commander Hardass. Maybe she'll demote me to something worse. Is there something worse?" Fecanya tapped her finger to her cheek. "Breath Fairy? Bunion Fairy?" She snapped her fingers. "Ah! Fungus Fairy. Surely there *must* be a Fungus Fairy!"

Fecanya zigzagged between her traveling companions in mock glee. "Now I understand why you were so insistent I magic up that gob of donkey doo we passed back in that pasture, Bloom! It could be so much worse."

The four fairies flew on wrapped in a quilt of charged silence for a while. Eventually, Fecanya felt her temperature lowering, and her frown started to smooth away. Sugressa caught up and glided beside her in silence for a time.

"You okay, Fecanya?" she finally asked. "I'm sorry."

"About what?" Fecanya asked with more steel in her voice than she'd intended. When Sugressa flinched, she angled over and gave the sugar fairy a quick hug. "I'm sorry. Didn't mean to snap."

"It's okay. I think you should be entitled to vent. Some of us have much more desirable jobs than others. Maybe we should restructure things, you know? Rotate the jobs. You should be able to make things sweet sometimes, and I should—"

"Stop right there, Sugressa." Fecanya smiled at her. "I appreciate what you're saying. The fact that you're genuinely willing to subject yourself to my job is the reason why your job is to make things sweet. It's who you are."

Sugressa smiled back at her. "I think that's the nicest thing you've ever said to me."

"You had to go and make it weird, didn't you, Cloy?" Fecanya said.

Sugressa grinned and shook her head. "You're nicer than you let on. I don't know why you want people to think you're so mean."

"Because I am mean," Fecanya replied, a shade of wistfulness creeping into her voice before she could stop it.

"You're not mean." Sugressa pressed her lips together. "Even when you're on a roll with your, er, sarcasm, it's never intentionally hurtful." She stole a glance at Fecanya. "I don't think so, anyway."

Fecanya sighed. "We're fairies. We have our jobs made to order for each individual." Fecanya twitched her lips to the side. "Might explain why our names are all so unimaginative. I mean, seriously."

Sugressa opened and closed her mouth, likely having something encouraging on the tip of her tongue before indeed thinking of all their names.

"I may find it nauseating at times," Fecanya went on, "but you have a sweet nature. You'd be wasted processing garbage or strengthening caffeine. I process shit, so—"

"Don't you dare."

Fecanya raised her eyebrows. That was new. *Girl's got a hard streak I've never seen before.*

"Don't you even *think* about yourself like that," an uncharacteristically steely Sugressa went on. "Just because you're an ordure engineer doesn't mean you have a shit personality." She slapped a hand to her mouth. "Oh no. By Lilith's Underworld! I've cursed. I've uttered a terrible term."

Three pairs of eyebrows rose, and the wide-eyed fairies glanced at one another. Garbita raised a fist to her mouth to hide her grin, and cleared her throat.

Seeing Sugressa's coloring cheeks darken, she zipped in a circle around her and pressed both hands to her cheeks. "Oh, whatever will happen now? All around the world, cakes and pies will grow sour! Berries and fruit will become spicy."

"That's not funny, Fecanya." Despite her indignant tone, Sugressa visibly relaxed. "I'm a sugar fairy. I'm not supposed to go around spewing foul language."

"Quiet, everyone." Bloomara held up her hand as she pulled to a stop. She peered down into the thick green woods below. Leafy trees rustled in a constant breeze upon which drifted the prattling of distant shrill voices.

"What is that, Bloomara?" Garbita asked.

"Talking. Lots of it." Bloomara frowned. "Yes. I do believe I hear talking. Lots and lots of talking. It sounds like many conversations all at once, tripping over each other."

Garbita wrinkled her nose. "Pointless chatter, you say? Perhaps we could fly over or around it."

"They may know something, whoever they are," Bloomara said. She gave a nod of finality. "Let's see what we can learn."

As the fairies flew on, the sounds of rampant and rapid conversation grew louder. Soon they found themselves amid a cacophony of chatter.

Sugressa pressed her hands over her ears. "This is torturous. What is all this?"

Fecanya, too, had her hands pressed over her ears. "Maybe we can magic up some muzzles. I feel like I'm going to lose my mind."

"Hey, guys! Check it out."

The hovering fairies turned in the direction of the baritone voice. A shining white bird with a large black hooked beak perched on a nearby branch above. It turned its head to the side to get a good look at them. The bird spread its wings and a patch of feathers lifted up on top of its head much like the roof of a human convertible car, but in the opposite direction. "Fairies, guys. We got fairies."

The words "Fairies! Hyah hyah!" echoed through the thick woods.

"Parrots," Fecanya said dryly.

"That cockatoo's voice sounds like a human singer—"

"Barry White," Garbita interrupted. When the other fairies looked at her, she cleared her throat. "Or so I've heard. Deep voice like ..." she waved her fingers at the parrot. "Like that one."

An African Gray glided out of the woods to land on a nearby branch. "You're cute," she said to Fecanya. She waved a wing in a circular gesture at her head. "Love the hair."

Fecanya reached back and patted the back of her head and smiled. "Oh yeah?"

Bloomara glided over. "Pardon me, Miss. Parrot—"

"Rrrrrrrrrrrrrrrrrraaaaaaaaaaaaaaaooooooooooooooorrrrrrrrrrrrrrrr."

Bloomara leaned away and started to drift backwards.

Fecanya glanced from the parrot to Bloomara as she, too, started to drift away when the parrot spoke again. "Is that its natural color, or did you get into the human dye? Like, I like my feathers and all," she lifted a wing. "But sometimes being gray with a little red at the tips can get boring, you know?"

"Uh huh," was all Fecanya could manage.

"It's too bad we can't magic stuff like you fairies," the parrot burbled on.

Bloomara tentatively glided closer again.

"If I had magic, I'd maybe turn my feathers purple rrrrrrrrrrrrrrrrrrraaaaaaaaaaaaaaaoooooooooooooorrrrrrrrrrrrrrrrr."

Bloomara glided back again.

"Or maybe even yellow or blue!"

Fecanya remained as still as possible as she watched the black, hooked pliers attached the front of the birds face opening and closing as she rambled on.

The Umbrella Cockatoo bounced his head. "Four fairies in the woods, just like—"

"Not quite finished." The African Gray deliberately swiveled on her branch to look at the cockatoo. "I think I was talking about something important, over here."

"Er," Fecanya ventured.

The African Gray swiveled back. "Don't mind SloMo over there. He's always rude."

"I am not always rude," SloMo argued. "Why do you always slander—"

"SloMo?" Sugressa asked.

"Short for SloMo Backslap," the African Gray said."

Sugressa glanced at Fecanya, who shrugged.

"How'd you get the name SloMo ... er ... Backslap?" Sugressa asked.

That brought on a round of laughter through the surrounding trees.

"I made the mistake of backslapping my human when he reached into my cage."

Fecanya's mouth wrinkled into a grin. "What was he trying to take?"

"Didn't get that far," the parrot answered in a voice that rumbled through Fecanya's chest cavity. "The fool reached into my house and I backslapped him. Kinda had to take off out the window after that." He shrugged. "And here I am hanging out with this hostile bird, over here."

"I am not hostile. I am a nice bird."

More laughter.

"Go ahead and tell 'em, Luca," a large blue parrot said.

Fecanya's teeth chattered at the loud, shrillness of the big bird's voice.

"I'm gettin' to that part, Dreyfus," the Luca said.

"Luca?" Fecanya said. "They named you Luca?"

"I named myself Luca," the African Gray said. "The Ashen Luca—"

Bloomara backed away again when The Ashen Luca descended into another deep, roaring growl.

"I think you should just stay away," Sugressa whispered loudly.

"Like I was saying," The Ashen Luca continued, eye on the left side of her head glaring at Bloomara. "My human put her fingers in front of me demanding I stand on them. I told her I wasn't standing on any hand with knuckles that ashy, and, well, you just don't talk to humans like that if you value not living in a lab and being tested for speech recognition for the rest of your life. So I took off."

"Then she bit me on the face and called *my* knuckles ashy, SloMo Backslap muttered."

"You are totally lying right now," The Ashen Luca replied.

"I think this is spiraling out of control," Fecanya whispered to Bloomara. "Um. By any chance, did you happen to see anyone strange pass through here?"

"Anyone strange?" Luca scratched the back of her head with a four-toed foot. "Well actually, we talked to a cat and he said—"

"Did you say cat?" Fecanya asked.

The Ashen Luca stood up straight, back arched, neck extended farther than any creature bound to the laws of physics should be permitted. She started hopping on her branch, bobbing her head up and down. "Hey guys. I think they ran into Muffinpie!"

"Who?" Fecanya asked. The beginnings of an insistent grin crept across her face despite her best effort.

"Orange and white Tabby?" Luca asked. "Prowls around north of here?"

"Oh, you mean *Diesel*," Garbita said.

"Diesel ..." Luca did a sort of penguin-like shuffle as she turned and looked back at SloMo, who stood statuesque on his branch. Luca then looked from SloMo to the big hyacinth macaw, Dreyfus. "Diesel." She looked at the surrounding parrots. "Guys. *Diesel!*"

"I know parrot facial features are pretty-much fixed," Sugressa whispered into Fecanya's ear. "But they look on the verge of hysterics."

Fecanya looked from tree to tree, populated by dozens and dozens of smirking parrots.

"He's calling himself Diesel, guys," The Ashen Luca said, her already high-pitched voice trembling with repressed mirth.

"Is that not his name?" Sugressa asked in her customary naive voice.

The dam broke.

All the fairies could do was hover in place, waiting for the laughter of dozens of parrots—doubled over or simply falling aside on their branches —to play out.

"Diesel?" A red, blue, and green macaw cackled. "Uh, no. His name is Muffinpie!"

The woods erupted to the laughing chorus of "MUFFINpie! MUFFINpie! Hyah hyah hyah. MUFFINPIE!"

"Muffinpie?" Garbita snorted, then joined the parrots. "That *insufferable* alley cat's *real* name is *Muffinpie*?"

Fecanya took a deep, trembling breath as she fought off convulsions of her own repressed laughter. On her left, Bloomara pretended to rub her bunching cheeks, while Sugressa looked around with a crinkled smile.

"Ahem." Fecanya flew a little closer to the African Gray named The Ashen Luca. "We're looking for someone who may have kidnapped our friends. Um," her voice trembled. Muffinpie told us—"

"MUFFINpie. MUFFINPIE! Hyah hyah. MUFFINPIE MUFFIN-PIE! Hyah MUFFINPIE!"

Fecanya cleared her throat. "Um. Okay guys it's not funny anymore." Several single-eyed stares leveled on her, making it clear the parrots didn't believe that lie any more than she did.

"Oookay," she tried again. "So ..." every parrot in sight leaned forward in anticipation. "Um ... yeah, so, the *cat...*" she raised her voice to be heard over the disappointed groans, "told us that someone scantily clad, with a sack over her back, passed through the forest headed this way. You know anything about that?"

"Actually, yeah," Luca responded. "Some lady with red hair, wearing leaves and vines for clothes and all that. The trees help her out, too." Luca shook herself to fluff up, her cheek feathers covering her lower beak. "I saw her from a distance, mind. Didn't want to get too close to that one. Had a look of mischief. Not to mention tree limbs and vines bending all around to hold stuff for her. I don't chirp with that kind of business."

Fecanya blinked. "Parrots don't chirp. You all kinda squawk."

Farther back above Luca, Dreyfus rose to her full height, bright blue belly pushed out. "We do *not* squawk. We project. How about *you* try to get your point across an entire forest."

"You're really pretty." Sugressa zipped up closer to the proud hyacinth and waggled a finger at her eyes. "It looks like you have yellow eyeshadow on. It contrasts so beautifully with your blue!"

"Why, thank you, my spritely friend." She raised a foot to pat the feathers at the back of her head. "I try not to squint in order to keep the yellow smooth, you know."

"It's lovely," Sugressa said. "Um, if you don't mind my asking, why's your name Dreyfus?"

Dreyfus dipped her head under the weight of her sigh. "The human family that handed over a bunch of those small, dirty flat green sheets to the people with whom I used to live, had a little boy. They let that smelly little lump name me."

"I ... see." Sugressa gave the macaw a comforting pat on the back.

Dreyfus sighed again. "It may get cold and rainy out here in the forest, but all of these miscreants have taught me how to survive, and find the nooks and crannies in the larger oaks where I can huddle in. Sometimes you end up with a squirrel family, but they're nice enough. I sometimes carry them to more distant patches of land with more nuts, and we share. It's a good, mutual agreement."

"Alrighty then." Fecanya clapped her hands together. If she didn't cap this off, Sugressa would have them here for hours. "We'd best be on our way, what with finding our abducted sistren and all. If you could point us in the right direction, we'll be off."

"That way." SloMo Backslap pointed a snowy white wing past them. "More east than south. If you're lookin' for your ... um, cisterns, and you think the vine girl's got 'em, that's where you're going."

The fairies turned in the direction the parrot pointed. As much as she tried, Fecanya couldn't keep from noticing that they were facing in the direction of a distant, snowcapped mountain. "Er, where?"

"That way!" SloMo barked, umbrella crest on his head raising ever-so-slowly.

Fecanya stared at the cockatoo while he continued to side-eye them. That eye, combined with the seemingly impossible beaky grin invoked about as much trust as a hyena's grin. "You're sure about that?"

SloMo cupped a scaly foot over his beak, much like a human might do to suppress a laugh. "Yup, sure," came the muffled response.

"Then, we go," Bloomara declared.

"Uh, Bloom," Fecanya said, still eyeing the cockatoo. "I think—"

"We can discuss it on the way, Fecanya," came the haughty response. "We've not the time."

"Better getcha going!" SloMo agreed, just a little too brightly, Fecanya thought. "Last we saw, she was headed around the remote side of the mountain. Humans call it Mount Baker, or some such. Look for Yeti Yack-obil. He'll know where she went."

"Bloom?" Fecanya tried once more.

"*Later*, Ordure Engineer," Bloomara snapped.

Many feathered heads swiveled to focus an eye on Fecanya. Those eyes said, "you really gonna take that?"

Fecanya looked at Bloomara, arms crossed over her chest. "Yes indeed, Head Fairy of Blooms. Lead on."

The fairies lifted higher into the air and zipped away to the tune of loud sniggering and shouts of MUFFINPIE!"

SEVEN

If her own magical nature wasn't keeping her warm enough, Fecanya was sure the heat from her irritation at Bloomara would have done the job. She glared at the head fairy's back. *How I'd love to slap that frozen blue bun off the top of her head.*

"Why can't we just pop through a portal to get there?" Sugressa yelled over the more loudly yelling winds.

"We must ensure we don't miss the abductress in case she's still traversing the mountain," Bloomara called back.

"I *have* my *doubts*, Bloomara," Garbita replied. Wisps of her green hair flapped across her forehead and around the even larger bun at the back of her head. "From the description those avian prats gave us, it sounded like the girls were kidnapped by a dryad. She wouldn't *be* up here."

"Whatever the case, we cannot take the risk of missing her just to avoid a little snow," Bloomara insisted.

"I'm sure we're almost there," Sugressa said, pointing at the distant peak.

Fecanya looked up to the snowcapped peak. It loomed over them like an incredulous badass, surprised that they hadn't frozen solid by now.

"Do you think there really is a Yeti Yackobil that lives up here?" Sugressa asked. "Or that the dryad came this way?"

"I'm absolutely certain she came this way," Fecanya replied. "I can't imagine a dryad choosing to go *anywhere* other than a sparsely wooded, snow-covered mountain. Where else in the heavily forested domain the humans call Washington, would she go?"

Bloomara's jaw tightened, but she remained silent.

They rounded a bend just in time to catch a sudden gust of snow. They took cover in a hollow at the base of a tree until the wind died down, then pushed on.

Fecanya found she didn't need to glare at Bloomara, for Garbita did enough of it for both of them. "If we keep on with this *folly*, I'm going to pull a *wing* muscle."

Sugressa powered on in dutiful silence, shooting Bloomara the occasional concerned glance. Another howling gust turned Bloomara sideways, right in view of another of Sugressa's concerned looks.

"I'm ... I'm sure we're almost there," she said in a confident—if strained—tone.

They followed a winding path through a lone, stubborn patch of trees where a solitary snowy owl perched. The owl swiveled its rocking head in their direction and barked a raspy hoot at them.

Sugressa flapped her hand in an excited wave at the hunkered down owl. "Hi there! You're really brave to be up here all alone when all your buddies are down at the base of the mountain."

Beak open midhoot, the owl blinked and slowly closed it. It swiveled its head in the direction Sugressa pointed, as though a great revelation had been dropped onto its head. After somewhat of an embarrassed silence, the owl took wing.

"Goodbye, friend!" Sugressa waved excitedly at the owl's back as it disappeared into the white void. "So strange." Sugressa looked to Fecanya, then back over her shoulder. "I've never seen an owl fly with its head hunched down like that."

"What's that?" Garbita pointed further up to the treeless trail where the snow-drowned woods finally gave up. "Looks like some sort of *snow* sculpture. *Quite* the *detail*. I think I shall have a closer look."

Fecanya resisted the urge to pat her street-smart deficient companion on the head. "I think that's our guy, Garbita."

"What? But he's *standing* so *still*."

"That's because I'm lookin' at a bunch o' fairies roughin' it in the middle of a snowstorm near the top o' this mountain, just afore winter."

The snow sculpture lifted a large, leathery hand that would put a gorilla's to shame. That random thought sent Fecanya's mind across the world, all the way into an African jungle. She wondered how King Leo and his Silverback Spartans were getting on.

Just the thought of that warm—if humid—jungle brought a bit of comfort in the midst of the surrounding snowscape. She hugged herself and looked around at the evergreen trees, their branches laden with snow. To ensure proper maintenance of the wintry tundra effect, a howling wind swept across a nearby lake and passed through the shivering woods farther uphill.

"I figured you all'd want someone to witness your final moments as you searched for a good spot to get buried and frozen," the big shaggy humanoid went on.

Bloomara's back stiffened and her cheeks puffed like an indignant blowfish. "I assure you, sir, that we are not searching for a place to expire."

The humanoid frowned his massive, overreaching unibrow at her. "Ain't said nothin' about no old groceries, fairy. I said you's lookin' like you're out here gonna die."

Fecanya flew to the front of the party while Bloomara hovered in cheek-trembling indignation. "We're looking for a Mr. Yeti Yackobil. Know where we can find one?"

"Yup. You got one right here." Yeti Yackobil thumped his massive, furry chest. "Dunno how many Yetis named Yackobil's livin' up this mountain, but since I'm the only one I'm aware of, it's gon' have to be me you're lookin' for."

"Nice to meet you, Mr. Yackobil!" Sugressa chirped.

Yackobil favored the sugar fairy with a somewhat scrunched smile. He looked at Fecanya while jabbing a thumb in Sugressa's direction. "She for real?"

Sugressa zipped up to Yackobil with wide-eyed wonder, fists pressed to her cheeks. "Your fur is SO white!" She looked up at him as she reached out a hand. "May I?"

Yackobil's protruding frown reversed itself to resemble terraces on the side a mountain with a receding tree line. "Sure thing, little lady." He puffed out his chest.

Sugressa reached out and plucked free a single follicle. "There! You had a single brown one there, throwing it all off. Now it's perfect!"

Yeti Yackobil's body barely shuddered. "M'thanks, little lady," he grunted through clenched teeth.

Bloomara glided over and directed Sugressa away. "Pardon, Mr. Yacko-bil, but have you a place we might talk?"

Yackobil looked around. "This ain't a place?"

"Erm, perhaps a place with shelter, Mr. Yackobil."

The towering yeti shrugged and turned away. "C'mon, then. Let's get'r goin'."

The fairies followed the marching giant closely, changing positions around him depending on the direction of the wind. Gusts of snow pounded them from one direction, then the next, but Yackobil seemed hardly to notice. The yeti provided enough of a barrier from the storm that Fecanya was willing to endure the close-range gaminess.

"Almost there." Yackobil pointed toward the top of the hill. "Gots a cave up there."

Fecanya, who'd unfortunately been flying near his armpit, wiped her watering eyes and nodded. "M'kay." She lurched ahead, practically galloping in the air to get away from the warm, moist—aged limburger-like —odor, and inhaled fresh snowy air.

The others came in right behind her, also gasping for sweet, fresh oxygen. Several moments later, Yackobil stomped into the cave just as Garbita whipped out her wand and magicked up a tidy campfire.

"Welp, this is it. Nice and warm for you little skinny types. Make your-selves comfortable!" Yackobil spread his arms in a welcoming gesture.

With timing only a practical sense of humor could produce, the wind changed direction and a breeze swept into the cave. It caressed every inch of Yeti Yackobil's armpits, then transported the odor through the campfire for added warmth before depositing it into the fairies' olfactory nerves.

"Oh my." Sugressa placed a finger under her nose.

"Oomph!" Fecanya's wings buzzed and she bolted—carefully around the yeti's underarms—straight for the cave exit. "Huuuuuuh!" She inhaled sweet frozen air until her lungs burned.

"Dear me, that is just *rancid*," Garbita croaked.

Fecanya looked on the other side of Garbita to see Bloomara on hands and knees, wheezing as the snow gradually built around her. Sugressa floated out of the cave, most of the color returning to her face.

"Figgerin' to just talk out here, then?" Yackobil asked. He stomped out of the cave, broad smile splitting his large furry face. "Don't blame ya. Can get kinda stuffy in there."

"Gufmrgh!" Fecanya slapped her hand over her mouth. "Ya that's it."

Sufficiently recovered, the fairies placed themselves a safe distance away from Yackobil's underarms, and Garbita produced another campfire.

Yackobil sat down and held his leathery hands out in front of the flames, toasting the grime on his palms to a nice flaky crust. "So, what'dya wanna talk about?"

"I was just wondering," Sugressa said just as Bloomara opened her mouth. "How come you're here. Don't yeti's live pretty far from here. Like, the Himalayas?"

Yakobil shrugged. "Don't see why folks can't relocate like anyone else. Wanted to see the world. Broaden my horizons and all that."

Sugressa pressed a finger to her lips as she thought that out. "But ... how would you get here? I doubt humans would fly you on their planes."

"Especially with that noxious odor," Garbita muttered.

"I gots connections," Yakobil said.

Bloomara cleared her throat.

Yakobil produced—from somewhere they didn't want to contemplate —something resembling a throat lozenge.

Fecanya had never seen Bloomara's eyes and lips press so tightly together as to wrinkle. Even her chin was pressed against her neck as she shook her head and leaned away from the proffered item.

Yakobil shrugged and put the lozenge away.

"Missing fairies," Bloomara breathed. "We've reason to believe some friends of ours have been abducted by a dryad and brought up this mountain."

"Dryad?" Yackobil's mouth turned down as he considered the word. "Ain't that like a nymph? They lives in forests, don't they?"

Fecanya snorted. Bloomara glared at her.

"Unless there's types of nymphs I ain't never seen afore," Yackobil went on. He rubbed his forehead, much like a sloth polishing an apple. "I guess there *could* be snow nymphs, but I ain't never seen one. Doesn't hold up to makin' much sense, you ask me. I feels like they'd prob'ly be kinda cold, considerin' they don't wears nothin' for keeping the chill off, far as I know—"

"Does that mean you've not seen them, Mr. Yackobil?" Bloomara punched in.

Yackobil reared back at the sharp words. "No needs to be so prickly, Miss Fairy. And, no. I ain't seen no nymphs up here. Although if'n I did, I'd prob'ly have a good laugh at her bein' so thick in the head as to come all the way up here to catch her freeze-to-death. Ain't nobody but me, animals with thick coats, and humans bored with livin' come all the way up to the top here. What got put in your mind that one would come this way?"

From the corner of her eye, Fecanya saw Bloomara eyeing her. She cleared her throat and began picking at her fingernails.

"A particularly loud company of parrots suggested—"

"Parrots?" Yackobil interrupted. From down west? The Ashen Luca, SloMo Backslap, and Dreyfus started a *company*? What's they gonna sell? What's a bunch o' parrots gonna do with a—"

"The *flock* of parrots suggested they came this way," Fecanya said when she trusted her voice not to crack. Much.

"Ah. Heheh." Yackobil's huge shoulders bounced. "Well, it certainly describes that ole bunch. They comes up here every summer. Fulla' jokes, that bunch. Hangin' out in the trees all hidden-like. Callin' down to hikers tellin' 'em 'just a little farther'. Makin' mountain lion sounds, stuff like that."

Even sent a couple humans up to my cave while I was here. Never heard a human make sounds like them buggers when they walked in. Spent as much time tryin' to throw each other at me as get away." He shook his shaggy head. "The Scumlord Parrot Gang of Central Washington, they calls themselves. Always up for laughs, that bunch."

"You're suggesting they sent us up here as a joke?" Bloomara replied, her tone as cold as the weather.

"More like I'm sayin' they sent you up this mountain for nothin' and if it weren't for the howling storm, you'd prolly hear 'em laughin' atcha from here."

"Well!" Fecanya threw her hands up in the air. "They sure fooled us! I mean, who could have possibly known that a *forest nymph* wouldn't opt to hike through a snowstorm up a mountain leading to ... no forest? They sure fooled us good."

Yeti Yackobil squinted at her. "You know, little sprite. I ain'ts the swiftest avalanche on the slope, but it sounds like you're dippin' a bit into the sarcasm."

Sugressa made a show of looking the cave over while Garbita settled for an upside-down smile and a nod.

Bloomara pressed on, determined to wring at least a drop of dignity out the situation. "So, what you're saying, Mr. Yackobil, is that you've not seen or been visited by a dryad possibly bearing prisoners of our kind?"

Yackobil shook his head. "Nope. Though I'm thinkin' you could be askin' that question without growlin' it out. Stands to reason we're just havin' a bit o' the conversation and all." He snapped his fingers. "Ah! Maybe because I've been loose with my manners!"

Fecanya exchanged puzzled looks with the other fairies as their yeti host thudded back into his musty cave. A few moments later he loped back into view bearing a small—to him—sack.

"Eeeeeh." He sighed. "Here we go."

Fecanya watched in growing terror as Yackobil reached into a dingy sack and produced a handful of dates. The things looked as if they shriveled before her eyes in an attempt to flee the dirt caked under his fingernails.

Yackobil dumped the dates in the snow, then reached back into his sack and pulled out what looked like a granola bar, two leathery apples, and a square yellow bar with powdered sugar on top.

"These is my favorite." He held it up delicately between thumb and forefinger for the fairies to see. "Lemon bars, they's called. Good little buggers. Oh, and—"

Fecanya's anxiety grew through the lengthening moments while the yeti rifled through his sack. What horrors would he pull out of that thing next?

"Yeah!" Yackobil held up a can with a picture of a coconut on the side. "Mmmm, HMM! You ever had a taste o' the coconut water?"

EIGHT

Fecanya appeared at the edge of the woods to a smiling Sugressa, Garbita studiously hunting for litter, and a fuming Bloomara. "It's about time," the head fairy said.

"I had to properly thank the guy for his hospitality, since you ordered such an abrupt departure, Bloom. It was rather ungracious to just magic ourselves away when he shared his lemon bars and coconut water with us." Fecanya offered a crinkled smile.

Bloomara's nostrils flared. "We should be on our way and not wasting time."

A rather colorful agreement popped into Fecanya's mind but she kept it to herself. There'd be plenty of time to remind her of this incident after the kidnapped fairies were safe.

"Speaking of lemon bars," Sugressa said as they took off. "Those were actually really good. I didn't have to sweeten them at all, and they had just the right consistency between the soft filling, the firm crumble crust on bottom, and the topping with the powdered sugar. The coconut water wasn't so bad either, despite being canned and all."

"I can't be*lieve* you ate from that grimy creature's *hands*," Garbita said. "There *must* have been a dozen *organisms* living in the grime under his fingernails *alone*."

Sugressa bit her bottom lip. "That's why I blew on it first. And it would have been rude to refuse his hospitality."

"It was *rude* of him not to *bathe* first," Garbita replied.

"I don't think there's anywhere to bathe up on that cold mountain, Garbita. And he could have just left us to search all day and night, too."

"Mmph." Garbita waved a dismissive hand. "He *stank*. His *hands* stank, his *fur* stank, and the terrible *effluvia* wafting from his mouth and underarms was the stuff of *poison*."

Fecanya watched as the garbage fairy descended into a full rant as they landed on the side of the highway.

"There's just no ex*cuse* for someone to harbor such *unwholesome* hygiene habits—"

A deafening roar like the sound of a gargling tyrannosaurus rounded a bend, followed by a giant, raised black pickup truck.

"WATCH IT!" Fecanya tackled Garbita from the side, at the same time thrusting her hand out for an extra magical push. Garbita "oomphed" in her ear as the two of them arced through the air.

Fecanya squinted her eyes shut against the shower of grass, while mud spattered over the grass to ensure a full-body coating.

They hit the ground in a tangle of grunts, curses, wings, and limbs while the sound of screeching tires and a revving engine hollered in their ears.

"What is the *meaning* of this?" Garbita rolled Fecanya off of her and hopped to her feet.

Fecanya groaned at her skinned knee and looked over her shoulder. The truck skidded through the soft shoulder of the highway and fishtailed its way back to the road in a spray of mud, grass, and gravel.

Bloomara created a transparent protective dome against the debris. Through the deluge of gunk, Fecanya caught sight of the license plate, "DudeBro 187" as the truck sped away.

"You two okay?" Sugressa asked as Bloomara dismissed the dome.

Fecanya stood and looked down at herself. Her once perfectly clean, stout, burlap dress was now covered in grass which clung to the moist mud coating underneath. Beside her, Garbita stood with fists clenched at her sides, her dress now matching her hair.

"Nope." Fecanya looked back at the rapidly diminishing truck. "Not gonna let this stand." She lifted into the air.

"We don't have time for reprisals," Bloomara called up as Fecanya rose higher. "That goes for both of you," she said when Garbita came up beside her. "We have a mission—"

Fecanya and Garbita shot away in a trail of fairy dust. Fecanya's wings buzzed in a blur that would make a hummingbird exhausted. Garbita flew beside her, fists still pressed at her sides, speeding like an angry garbage-collecting missile.

The driver must have pressed the accelerator, for DudeBro 187 belched a black cloud at the two fairies.

"Sounds like the stupid thing is gargling," Fecanya yelled.

"Bleh!" Garbita sped out front and brandished her wand.

Fecanya surged forward as well, building her magic from within.

DudeBro 187 veered close to the shoulder of the road again launching another gravel assault. Fecanya swerved left, while Garbita went right. The motor gargled again, spewing more black engine phlegm.

"I've had *enough* of this hairless *ape!*" Garbita howled. She spun her wand in a circle, the end creating a sparkly magic trail. "Urgh!" She pointed the tip of her wand toward the truck's tailpipe. It coughed but kept going.

Fecanya noticed a seagull lazily gliding overhead and she lifted up into the sky. The seagull looked over at her with an expression the equivalent of an arched eyebrow. "Yeah?"

"Hey, there." Fecanya pointed down at the obnoxious black truck. "Mind doing me a favor and—"

"Say no more." The seagull flapped her wings and lifted higher into the air.

It's like they live for it, Fecanya thought. She dove down beside Garbita again. "Aerial assault incoming."

Garbita looked to the sky. "What ... oh. Oh!"

They backed off to a safe distance and watched as the seagull sped down toward DudeBro187 like a human fighter jet. She let out a loud screech that seagulls loved to do, even when nobody's around, then lifted up.

"That's ... quite the payload," Garbita remarked. As DudeBro 187 swerved left to right, the driver obviously blinded by the fully covered windshield.

Fecanya shuddered. "Looks like a couple days' worth of payload."

With a magical burst much like releasing a coiled spring, they shot forward and reached the truck again. Garbita caught sight of some road-side garbage and flicked her wand. The detritus jerked into the air and trailed her like the tail of a comet. With another flick of her wand, she sent the speeding refuse streaming into the yawning tailpipe of the truck.

Dudebro 187 changed lanes to avoid a chunk of rubber left from a semi, which Fecanya promptly scooped up with a bit of magic. She broke it up into long strips and sent the debris flying under the truck and up into the engine.

BOOOOOM clacklacklackalcklacklack. Loud and impressively crafted expletives filtered between the seams of the upraised windows as Dudebro 187 lurched toward the side of the road.

Fecanya zipped underneath the truck, but kept a safe distance from the oil filter. She waved her hands in the air, magical sparkles trailing her gestures. The oil filter burst, and oil vomited out of the engine.

Garbita swept her wand around in an upward arc, and the oil leveled out before it touched the road.

Flying sideways and giggling the whole way, Fecanya waved her hands in circular motions, which Garbita imitated with her wand.

The black substance attached to the asphyxiating truck's tires and caramelized into a smooth black coating. Dudebro 187 slid onto the shoulder of the road and stumbled into the brush, bouncing and bucking like an angry stallion.

The truck's tailgate dropped open like an incredulous bottom lip, while Fecanya sped around to the front windshield. She waggled her fingers and waved her hands. A shower of magic sparkles settled over the wind-shield and solidified the results of the avian assault. She snickered at the sound of cursing from inside the truck and zipped around behind it.

Having collected all of the soil and gravel that had been coated with the oily tires Garbita now carefully deposited it into the gas tank.

They returned to see Sugressa making an effort not to look amused, and Bloomara tapping her foot. "Your disobedience is shameful, Fecanya. Not shocking, but shameful nonetheless." She looked to Fecanya's accomplice. "And you. I would have expected better, Garbita."

Garbita stared at the ground and wrinkled her chin. "That *human* was a donkey's *ass*, Bloomara. He mustn't have been allowed to go un*punished*."

Fecanya looked Bloomara in the eye, silently daring her to claim she wouldn't have done something similar, had that truck nearly flattened her instead of Garbita.

Bloomara broke off contact first and cleared her throat. "What if you'd been seen?" she asked Garbita. "That was a reckless venture."

"Could've wiped his memory of us," Fecanya offered.

"You also could have harmed the human, or caused an accident. You could have caused harm to a good number of trees and animals as well. *And* you know we don't go around wiping human memories unnecessarily, Fecanya. There is no excuse for your irresponsible behavior. Either of you."

As much as she'd have rather bathed in a bed of lava, Fecanya couldn't deny that Bloomara was right. *Ugh.* "Look ... yeah ok you're right. I'm so—"

"I'll hear no more!" The side of Bloomara's mouth twitched. It was no more than a flicker, but Fecanya caught it. "Just ... we need to move. No more shenanigans!"

If they weren't supposed to not like each other, Fecanya might have thought about maybe not throwing up if she'd hugged Bloomara. She settled for mumbling out a "yeahsureokay."

The fairies followed Bloomara into the air. Fecanya and the others pretended they didn't hear Bloomara snort around her efforts to hide her grin.

Beside Fecanya, Sugressa winked.

NINE

"I don't think I've ever seen that many humans in such a dour mood," Sugressa said.

Fecanya looked back at the rapidly diminishing suburb below. "What makes you say that? Don't all humans greet each other by way of fistfight and fender bender? Remember the lady we saw leaving the coffee shop? She combined both in one." She smirked. "That uppercut would have done King Leo proud. She lifted that guy clean off his feet."

The mention of King Leo, leader of the Silverback Spartan Gorillas brought a smile to Fecanya's face. She really did need to go back and visit them, one day.

"It really is unusual, Fecanya," Sugressa said. She shook her head, stray pink strands of hair blowing across her face. "They're so angry."

"*When* are humans *not* angry?" Garbita asked. "Angry is what they *do*. They leave it *every*where, like a stench."

Sugressa's brow furrowed at that. "I don't think that's true, Garbita. There are lots of humans that are kind. Remember that wedding I serviced?" She beamed at the thought. "The cake was good, but I touched it up juuuust a bit right. It was a hit!"

"The bride and groom took a gob of it in each hand and rammed it into each other's faces," Fecanya replied, her tone as dry as the pita chips at the wedding.

"It's a tradition, Fecanya. You know that."

Fecanya nodded. "Yup. A hostile one. I mean, only a human would think to assault their brand-new mate with food merely seconds after being joined." She angled over and elbowed the sighing Sugressa, drawing a giggle.

The fairies came to another patch of human civilization along the highway and glided in. As soon as they touched down on the roof of a "We've Got Ya Covered" insurance building, Fecanya noticed a crowd collecting in front of a building down the street. "Hey, Bloom. Check it out." She pointed at a shop named "Camren's Coffee Corner".

"Everyone remain invisible and follow me," Bloomara ordered.

Fecanya rolled her eyes as the bloom fairy lifted and took off.

"Can't *imagine* that I would have thought of such a thing without in*struction*," Garbita muttered.

Fecanya let out a guffaw before she could stop herself. She started coughing when Bloomara looked over her shoulder.

They passed several humans ranging from dazed to semiconscious to flat-out irritable. One man stomped by, reusable coffee mug caving in under the pressure of his hairy-knuckled grip.

A dog looked at the passing invisible fairies and slobbered in greeting, while a Siamese cat perched on a fence looked at them as if to say, "you're not fooling anyone."

Not far away from the smug feline a gaggle of altercating humans quickly descended into pushing and forehead shoving.

"Oh my." Sugressa held a hand over her mouth and pointed at the arguing primates. "They're going to harm each other."

A human wearing a blue full-body apron and matching cap walked out of Carmen's Coffee Corner and held his hands up in the air. The crowd gathered around.

"Everyone, I'm sorry, but we've only got enough Power Roast for ten more cups. But we do have a *lot* of decaf left."

Lots of teeth bared at that last bit.

"What the hell are we supposed to do with decaf?" One human asked. He thrust his palms in the air and his paperboy cap nearly fell of the back of his head. "Bathe in it?"

Another human sporting a pair of dingy green trousers held up by matching suspenders and a grocery bag-brown shirt nodded. The multilayered bags under his eyes did a fine job of punctuating his irritation. "Come to think of it, why does decaf even exist? That's like drinking dry water."

"That makes absolutely zero sense," a woman next to him said. Even her blue dyed ponytail was stiff with annoyance. "Dry water? If it's dry, it ain't water."

"My point exactly," Dingy Trousers said.

"But decaf coffee's still coffee," Angry Ponytail shot back. "Dry and water can't be the same thing."

"Don't remember talkin' to you at all," Dingy Trousers snapped.

"Yeah, but if I don't stop you now, you'll suck up all the good oxygen and exhale false equivalencies that smell like garlic and pork skins."

"Why don't you mind your own business?" the man said.

"Why don't just shut that muffin-mangler under your nose so we can find out our options," another man said. He rubbed his bloodshot eyes and glared at Dingy Trousers and Angry Ponytail.

"People, please. Please!" The barista waved his hands in the air. "I know it's frustrating, but we've used our distributor for years. The coffee beans have come from the same place, but this latest shipment has been weak on caffeine. We also have tea—"

"Do I look like I drink tea?" a young man asked. He scratched his head, disrupting the nest of dandruff in his man-bun.

"You don't smell like you bathe, either," a younger woman quipped, "yet there's soap and water available."

"Uh oh," Sugressa said as they watched the arguing intensify.

Fecanya shoved her amusement aside. "I'm guessing Caffeinisa is missing?" When Sugressa nodded, Fecanya whistled through her teeth. "Oooh yeah. This is going to be good. Without Caffeinisa, a good chunk of the greater Seattle area is going to be in chaos."

"You have a *questionable* concept of "good", Fecanya," Garbita remarked.

Fecanya waved a hand to encompass the barking humans. "You telling me that's not worth of at least *one* box of popcorn? I mean, c'mon, Garbita. A bunch of primates arguing over coffee. It's fantastic."

"This is worse than I thought," Bloomara said. "Tootheria *and* Caffeinisa have been kidnapped. We must find their abductor and quickly, before this escalates."

"What's the worst that can happen?" Fecanya said. She looked back down at the now jostling crowd. They looked like tall, clothed chimpanzees shoving at each other over hot and bitter drinks."

"Oh, I can't *imagine* what could happen when enough *humans* start fighting," Garbita said. "*Surely* there isn't an apocalyptic *precedent* for such a thing."

When a man wearing a velvet blazer and sweatpants bit another man on the wrist for touching him, the fairies figured it was time to go. They lifted off of the rooftop, leaving behind a growing cacophony of under-caffeinated bickering.

TEN

"Yup," Fecanya whispered. They watched from behind a gnarled old oak as a woman shoved the pointy end of a scone up another woman's nose during a tug-of-war over the last cup of Strong Bound Hyperdrive Roast. "I hate to admit it, Garbita, but you're right. They're going to start damaging themselves and eventually everything else."

"Got that right," said a voice from above. Fecanya looked up to see a sloth making his way down the tree. "Just hold on and I'll tell you all about it."

"Gonna be a while, then," Fecanya muttered.

Garbita frowned. "A sloth? In North America?"

"Yup," the sloth said. "Some humans got hold of me back in my home some years ago. Ended up living in a house with a parrot. Didn't much like it, though the food was good. Ended up conspiring with the parrot to break out."

"I must *admit*, my good sloth," Garbita said. "I'd be very *interested* in how you *managed* that."

"We don't have the days it would take for that story to play out, Garbita." Bloomara coaxed the nearby leaves to arrange themselves into little chairs and a table.

Garbita responded with a disappointed shrug, but magicked up a full high tea setup.

"You know what?" Fecanya took a sip. "These little sandwiches are pretty doggon good, Garbita. I'm telling you," she took another sip, then shoved a sandwich in her mouth. You've got a talent, here. You could sell these things."

"To *whom*?" Garbita asked. "You *know* fairies don't use *money*, Fecanya."

"But humans do," Fecanya replied. "I'm sure you could magic up a front and sell these things for a mint."

Garbita blinked at her, then looked off into the distance. "You know, that *might* be an *idea*."

"And what, pray tell, would you do with a bunch of dyed and treated sheets of paper, exactly?" Bloomara asked. She looked up to see that the sloth was nearly halfway to them.

"Humans seem to get on well enough using them," Garbita said, the wheels in her mind still turning."

"I don't know what's worse," Bloomara replied. "The fact that they trade paper sheets for things they *don't* need, or the things that they *do*. And it's paper, Garbita. *Paper*."

"It has worth to them," Garbita offered, the strength in her argument beginning to fracture.

Bloomara picked up leaf. "Here. I'll give you two of these every day if you'll come clean my pod and make me high tea."

Garbita stared at the proffered leaf. "What would I do with a *leaf*, Bloomara?"

"The same thing you'd do with a sheet of paper," Bloomara stated. "This leaf is worth a room cleaning. One more is worth high tea."

Even the bun on top of Garbita's head seemed to frown at that. "Says who?"

"Says me," Bloomara said.

"That makes no sense," Garbita replied.

"Why not?"

"I ... because." Garbita deflated a little more. "But—"

"I think she's right," Fecanya said, coming to the rescue despite her better judgement. "If you try to do anything like a human, you'll wind up insane."

They enjoyed the remainder of the tea, sandwiches, and biscuits, Sugressa sprinkling a bit of sweetness to give them a little more kick.

"Alrighty, then," the sloth said, half an hour later.

The fairies jumped at the sound of his voice, and glanced at each other. "I kinda forgot we were waiting for him," Sugressa whispered in Fecanya's ear.

"Greetings, good sloth," Bloomara said. "You were going to speak to us about that human scuffle?"

"Yup," the sloth said. He reached up and adjusted his greening brown headband and legwarmers, then pulled his jogging shorts up. After stamping his feet—presumably to get the blood flowing—he yanked the wrinkles out of his brown, polyester jersey. "You're lucky, you are. Caught me at a good time."

He turned toward a gravel trail snaking through the woods, the wrinkles returning to his jersey while the multi creased paper number two resumed its dangling position on his back. "I was heading down the tree for a jog. You're going to have to come along if you want the news. I have to keep my workout schedule, you understand."

"Of ... course, good sloth," Bloomara replied.

"No need to be so formal," the sloth said, leaning forward. "Name's Arthur Carnevale Cruzindream."

"Er ... nice to meet you, Arthur Carnevale Cruzindream."

"Likewise," Arthur said as he started away. "Those humans are at each other's throats because the coffee's been weak. Been fighting here and there for about a week, now." He lurched forward and took a step.

"We've seen other towns in a similar state," Bloomara replied.

"Word around the trees is that someone's kidnapped the caffeine fairy." Arthur made a tsking sound. "Sucha shame. I met her once. Just being around her gave me enough pep to get in my fastest jog ever."

"Oh, you've met her?" Sugressa said. "Caffeinisa?"

"That's the one," Arthur said. "Such a lovely fairy. All zippy, like."

"She is quite lovely," Sugressa agreed.

"Mhmm." Arthur Carnevale Cruzindream took a second step, really leaning into his sprint. "She got me moving outta that unfair stereotype we sloths get. Not all of us is slow, you know."

"Um, Mr. Arthur Carnevale Cruzindream?" Sugressa said. "May I ask why you're out jogging?"

"Yup, you can ask," Arthur replied. "And since you practically did just now, no need to go askin' again. I'm training." He took a solid minute between steps to reach over his back, indicating the rumpled number two still hanging on to his back. "Training for a half marathon. Got'sta be in tip-top shape if I'm gonna win this thing!"

Fecanya nodded politely as the sprinting sloth inched away. "Any ideas on what might have happened to her?"

"Might possibly," Arthur wheezed. "I seen some young gal slinking around in the woods. I said to myself, I said, 'you know, ole Arthur Carnevale Cruzin? That gal looks mighty suspicious. Yup. Mighty suspicious.' So I took my time and climbed down to a lower branch to get a closer look."

"Did you make it to your *branch* in time to get that closer *look*, Mr. Cruzin?" Garbita asked.

"Don't remember giving anyone permission to call me by my nickname," Arthur muttered. He took another step. "I always thought nicknames was for folks that're familiar with you. Like friends and all that. But I guess things is all kinds of different, now."

"I ... didn't *mean* to *offend*, good sloth." Then, after a long silence in which all figured Arthur didn't plan to answer the question, Garbita tried again. "Did you *manage* to get to your *branch* in time to get a better look?"

"Can't think of a reason why I wouldn't have," Arthur replied. "I'm pretty limber and quick, you know."

Fecanya was sure she could hear laughter coming from the algae on Arthur's back, at that statement.

"I settled down ... what the heck are we talking about, again? Was it about that weird fungus grew in my ears last month? Took me something like an hour to pick it out."

Garbita's response was something between a gasp and a heave.

"Uh, I don't think we were talking about that," Fecanya said, ignoring her own nausea. "We're trying to find out—"

"Do you have any idea what that *smells* like?" Arthur Cruzindream went on.

Garbita's face turned a waxy green hue. "I'm going to be sick."

"Our kidnapped friends, Mr. Cruzindream," Bloomara said. "You were about to tell us about their kidnapper, whom you observed from the trees?"

"Oh, yes of course!" He took another step. "The young gal had a sack over her shoulder. Could'a sworn when she dropped it on the ground, I heard an 'oomph' that sounded just like Caffeinisa. You get to talking to a person long enough, you learn their voice. Mind you, I've never heard her go 'oomph' around me, but you hear a person's voice enough, don't matter if she says 'oomph,' or 'damn the torpedoes'."

Arthur Cruzindream took yet another step, this time inside of a full minute since his last step. His perpetual smirk-smile widened in self-satisfaction. "So I heard that 'oomph', and I thought to myself, I thought, 'Cruzindream, you speedy bastard. You need to get yourself down there and make sure your buddy Caffeinisa isn't in that there sack'."

His grin faded. "Unfortunately, the young lady up and took off before I could confront her. Must've used some way of magic to hurry on out before I could get to her."

Fecanya arched an eyebrow at the sloth. "Surely."

"What did she look like?" Bloomara asked before Arthur could find another tangent.

After ten seconds whereby Cruzindream completed his responding shrug, he began to indicate his own furry—and quite musty—body. "She was dressed a little too scantily if you asks myself. All skin, leaves, and vines. Could catch herself a fungus like that, she can. Especially the ones that go—"

"Uuh HEM, well yes, thank you," Bloomara interrupted. "Could you point us in the direction the lady went?"

"Sure can." Arthur pointed south toward Seattle. "Headed straight that way. Can't imagine why she'd be off to a big ole human civilization like that. Hard enough stayin' unnoticed in the small towns. She won't find nothing but trouble in a hurry, there."

He spent some time rubbing his chin. "Mind you, she's not an animal, so she doesn't have to worry about being eaten. I've seen my share of humans in the woods from up in the trees. I'll tell ya; the first thing a human says when they see anybody who ain't human, it's 'good eatin'.' You ever find yourself spotted by a human, first thing they're gonna say to their companion is 'now that there is good eatin'."

ELEVEN

Fecanya stole another glance at Sugressa. She'd been quiet ever since they left the male human squirming on the ground in an alley next to a yoga studio. "There's nothing we could do for him, Sugressa. You can't really magic away something like that."

The nymph had been easy enough to follow, once they'd heeded Cruzindream's advice and headed further south. The trail had been easy enough to pick up. The nymph had left a string of human misery that zigzagged from behind a department store in the nearly dead Everett Mall, southeast to Fobes Hill, to all the way southwest next to a dumpster beside a Burgers n' Brewha in Mukilteo. They'd found hidden humans, discretely squirming due to poison ivy exposure, or—as with the fellow they'd not been able to help—worse.

Sugressa sighed. "I know. But I feel like we could have done something. He just kept scratching and scratching. And all those little hair follicles growing on his tongue. That must have been so uncomfortable."

Fecanya pressed her lips together until she was sure she'd stifled her snort. "Well, he had that coming. It's a well-known fact that kissing a dryad when invited may or may not yield a human a pleasurable experience or a deadly one. But trying to French kiss one uninvited yields a hairy tongue, guaranteed."

"But how's he gonna breathe?" Sugressa asked.

"Well, he's not going to suffocate, if that's what you're worried about." Fecanya looked ahead, the tears of repressed laughter clouding her vision. "It's just going to ..." her voice cracked, "be a little uncomfortable, that's all. Probably tickle his throat and the roof of his mouth till the magic wears off."

"Oh dear." Garbita pointed out a patch of woods below. "There's another one."

"And another," Bloomara added, pointing ahead. "Farther on."

The fairies magicked themselves invisible and dove below the treetops. Yet another man lay squirming on the ground, scratching his arms, legs, and other places. Fecanya clicked her tongue at him as they drifted by. They found a woman in a similar condition a few hundred feet away, though the tube of lotion she had handy in her purse seemed to be helping.

"This dryad has quite the mischievous streak," Garbita said.

"I'll say," Fecanya replied. "Looks like she's making out with every human she comes across in the woods." She sniggered.

Bloomara waggled her finger. "This isn't funny, Fecanya."

"Yes, it is," Fecanya replied, to which Bloomara just sighed.

What first was an occasional human, thrashing in itchy torment, turned into a trail of them. Men and women lay scattered in woods and behind gas station carwashes, scratching arms, legs, hair, backs. "That guy must be a contortionist," Fecanya observed as they passed a man who had practically folded himself into a pretzel to get at the middle of his back.

"Yeti Yackobil and Cruzindream said the woman wore leaves and vines," Sugressa reminded. "Poison ivy?"

Fecanya nodded. "Has to be." She looked down at a male crouched over his ripped shirt behind a dumpster. "Poor bastards."

"How did the poison ivy penetrate all that hair, I wonder." Sugressa waved a finger at the squatting man, eyes clamped shut, teeth gritted as he raked his fingers up and down his hairy chest.

They passed a tractor shop where a man leaned against the corner of a brick wall. He groaned as he raised and lowered himself, grinding his back against the gritty surface. A few blocks away, a woman tore off the cap to a bottle of hand lotion and began slathering it all over her arms, under her shirt, on her face and in her hair.

"Could be worse," Fecanya said. "At least this dryad is just having a little bit of poison ivy fun. She could be leading them to her tree for more lethal activities."

"It's *more* than that," Garbita replied. "No ca*ffeine* in the *coffee*. No one to visit children to *collect* the *teeth*. Now we have itchy humans."

"The only thing more dangerous than a bored human," Bloomara said, "is an angry one."

A scratching man in denim overalls and a black shirt with a musket on the front tore the door to a nearby shed open and grabbed a metal rake.

"I think they're right, Fecanya," Sugressa said in a quiet voice. She flinched at the screams of the man in overalls. "I don't think we want to live on a world with angry, under-caffeinated, itchy, humans."

"They'll *wreck* the *world* right quickly," Garbita agreed.

The fairies followed the zigzagging trail of tormented humans from one town to the next, and through patches of woods in the evergreen state of Washington. After a stop just south of Everett, where traffic had backed up due to a number of humans wandering into the streets—scratching themselves like itching zombies—Fecanya heard a sound that made her wings quiver. "Did you hear that?"

"Hear what?" Bloomara asked.

"Giggling." Fecanya looked around. "Tiny voices giggling."

"Per*haps* your overactive imagi*nation*, Fecanya," Garbita replied.

"I'm serious, garbage girl," Fecanya snapped. "I've heard it before. If I'd ignored it then, we'd still be cleaning up the aftermath of that wastewater plant."

"No, *you'd* be cleaning up the aftermath, Ordure Engineer," Garbita shot back.

"I suppose I could use that giant bun sitting on your head," Fecanya offered. "It'd make a fantastic mop—"

"I think I just heard it," Sugressa said.

"What?" Fecanya looked over her shoulder. "I didn't hear anything."

"Because you were too busy talking to Garbita," Sugressa replied diplomatically. "But I heard it."

Fecanya knew for certain no giggling had happened. When she looked at Sugressa, the sugar fairy didn't meet her eye. Fecanya couldn't help but chuckle to herself. She never knew why Sugressa disliked when she and Garbita went on a row.

"Wait, I think I heard it, now," Bloomara said.

Fecanya heard again, too. Distant, subtle, and hair-raising. The wide-eyed fairies looked around the woods, but there was no one to be seen. "What does it mean?" Bloomara asked her.

"How would I know?" Fecanya replied. "I can only guess that it means the imps found another way to break through into this world like before."

"It's like they're trying to break out of jail to come here and stink up this world," Bloomara said, wrinkling her nose.

"Would you want to live in theirs?" Fecanya asked.

"But it's *their* world," Bloomara answered. "The dark world is where they're born and thrive. It just vexes me that they want to come here and ruin what we've got."

"Well ..." Garbita folded her arms. "You *do* realize that they want to get here because they are *genetically* related to *humans*."

"That's a rumor and you know it," Bloomara snapped.

"It's widely known," Garbita replied calmly, holding out a hand as if to hold her point in it. "They are so *similar*. Surely you can see that." She made an offhand gesture at Fecanya. "Even *she* can understand such a concept."

"But, demons and devils just want to wreck stuff," Sugressa said as they continued on. She discretely magicked up a cinnamon bun beside and slightly behind a human curled in the fetal position. Fecanya arched an eyebrow at Sugressa, who glanced at Bloomara and held a pleading finger to her lips.

"And humans don't?" Garbita asked.

"Not on purpose," Sugressa said. "They just kinda stumble into wrecking stuff. It's not the same thing."

Fecanya shrugged. "Semantics, Cloy. For example." She waved a hand toward Garbita's head. "If I were to stumble and accidentally turn that giant cinnamon bun into a coiled viper, would it be the same thing as if I actually meant to do it? The end result is the same." She held the tips of her fingers over her heart and haughtily closed her eyes. "The poor *viper* has to *live* with the *results*."

Sugressa choked back a snort and carefully looked past the glowering Garbita.

Bloomara coughed.

Garbita rounded on her, teeth bared. "Youuuuuu go *right* ahead and *try* it, shit fairy! I'll turn that *potato* sack you wear into a used *diaper* from one of those smelly *babies* whose *teeth* you pull."

Fecanya turned a circle, her palms facing the sky and her head wobbling. "Whose *teeth* you pulleh. The tooth fairy doesn't pull teeth, garbage girl. And babies don't have teeth to give Tootheria—"

"Yeeeeeeuw twinkle-nosed twit!"

Fecanya rocked back at that. She cupped a hand over her mouth in mock offense. "That was positively *ghastly* of you!" She turned to Bloomara and made her bottom lip tremble. "Hey, Bloom. I want to file a grievance. She called me a twinkle-nose."

"You can fill out the proper paperwork when we return to the facility," Bloomara replied.

They passed out of the human town and back into the woods, shedding their invisibility as they passed safely into the foliage.

"But my feelings are hurt now," Fecanya pressed, making her voice crack. "I mean, between being called a twinkle-nose, having to look at that croissant roll on her head, and being constantly assaulted by some weird version of "the queen's English", I don't know how long I can go on."

"That's *it*!" Garbita wailed. Her flaring nostrils made a good show of matching the size of her widened eyes.

"You gonna challenge me to a duel?" Fecanya asked.

"I'm going to *punch* your *lights* out!"

"I don't have any lights." Fecanya pointed at a streetlight below. "But you can punch that."

Garbita balled her fists.

Bloomara sighed.

Sugressa hovered between Fecanya and Garbita, hands outstretched. "Please, stop. We don't have time for this. Please."

"She started it," Fecanya muttered.

Garbita crossed her arms and lifted her chin. "I most *certainly* did *not*."

"Actually, you did," Bloomara grudgingly admitted.

"I did *not*!" Garbita insisted.

"You kinda did, Garbita," Sugressa said. She offered a sheepish smile. "But it doesn't matter—"

"Yes, it does," Fecanya said. "Means I can—"

"Forget about it and move on," Bloomara declared. "That's exactly what it means. If you two," she jabbed a finger at Fecanya and Garbita, "want to have a dustup, do it on your own time. I'll not have your nonsense interfering with this errand."

A voice quite unfamiliar slipped into the conversation. "And what, pray tell, is that errand, little sprite?"

TWELVE

The other three fairies jumped, while Fecanya pretended she wasn't having a near heart attack from being caught off guard. She even managed to keep her arms from trembling as she crossed them and planted a fractured grin on her face. "Well, well. Our quarry comes to us." She hoped no one noticed her voice crack.

A woman dressed in nothing but vines sporting expertly-placed leaves put her hand on her hip and stared at Fecanya. "Your voice cracked."

"Sore throat. Got a lozenge?"

"No. Do those things cure trembling, too?"

Fecanya waved a shaky dismissive hand. "Whatever."

The forest nymph snorted. "All right, let's get on with it. Why am I 'your quarry'?"

"You very well *know* the *reason* of our pur*suit* of you," Garbita snapped. "*Where* have you *taken* the other *fairies*?"

The forest nymph stared at her a long time before she finally blinked. Then, hand still on her hip, she looked at Fecanya and jabbed a thumb at the Detritus Distribution Fairy. "What's her schtick? Talking like a cheese connoisseur from '*across* the *ponnnduh*?"

Garbita balled her fists. "You are an *insolent* little *twit*!"

The nymph sniffed. "You smell like garbage—"

"I do *NOT* smell—"

Fecanya and Sugressa dove at the garbage fairy and just managed to grab her arms.

"Let me *go*!" Garbita gnashed her teeth, twisting around to try to get at the snickering nymph.

"C'mon, Garbita," Fecanya said. Despite fighting her urge to laugh, Fecanya truly didn't want to see Garbita get pummeled by the much larger nymph. "Let's keep it ladylike."

Bloomara drew herself up to her full haughtiness. "Assuming you truly are ignorant of our intentions, dryad, we've come for our sistren, whom you've abducted. We demand their immediate release and that you submit yourself for inquiry and fey justice."

A thin, wrinkled line creased the nymph's face and, once again, she looked to Fecanya. "She's for real?"

"Um, yeah," Fecanya said, her voice bouncing as her body jerked back and forth while restraining Garbita. "Look, all melodrama aside, you did kidnap our friends. We want them back and you need to answer for it."

The nymph poked out her bottom lip. "You four are no fun at all. Have you not *seen* what humans do when they can't get coffee in the morning? You lot," she waved a hand at them, "perform a lot of duties that make life more convenient for those primates, and they don't even believe you exist! All I'm doing is having a little fun."

"Causing problems for others is not fun," Bloomara declared. "It is mischief, and it will not be tolerated."

The nymph tilted her head at Bloomara. "Why is it your teeth show every time you speak. It's like you're chewing on toffee—"

"Stop changing the subject, nymph!" Bloomara shouted.

"My name is Siraka."

"Well ... then ..." Bloomara cleared her throat and tried again. "Stop changing the subject, Siraka!"

"Not enough entendre," Siraka instructed. She held the tips of her fingers and thumb together in front of her face. "You need to speak with more entendre. Project. You must project the entendre!"

"I speak with plenty of entendre, thank you very much," the indignant head fairy proclaimed.

Garbita stopped struggling and looked at Fecanya, who shrugged and let her go. Fecanya watched as Garbita turned to face the argument. "Do *either* of you actually *know* what you're talking about?"

"I know that bun at the top of your skull wobbles almost as much as your head when you talk," Siraka said.

The shadows of the nymph's makeshift prison chamber watched jealously as Garbita's angry visage put them to shame.

"You *really* need a good *thrashing*!" Garbita shouted.

"And you kinda warble when you're talking," Siraka went on. "Kinda like a turkey?"

"Says the insufferable *git* whose name sounds like a human *condiment*!" Garbita shot back.

"I bet you learn a lot about condiments while shopping through trash," Siraka countered.

"I. Don't. Shop. Through. *Trash*!" Garbita balled her fists again.

Fecanya forced a neutral expression on her face and zipped between them. "Look, I'm really, *really* enjoying this, but we actually do need to get back to business. You've kidnapped our friends and caused too many problems for humans." She spread her hands. "Can't say I don't know how fun that actually is, but you've taken it too far—"

"Wait." Siraka pointed at her. "Aren't you that shitty fairy I've heard about?"

Mouth still open midspeech, Fecanya blinked. "The official title is Ordure Engi—"

"Shit Engineer."

"Does that mean I should be engineering *you*?" Fecanya asked.

Siraka leaned back in mock intimidation. "Ooh, a comeba—"

"I mean," Fecanya went on, "I do specialize in it." She looked Siraka up and down. "So I know *shit* when I see it."

The nymph narrowed her eyes.

From her periphery, Fecanya saw Garbita slowly circling around the rapidly angering nymph.

"I think Sriracha's getting upset," Fecanya said to Sugressa.

"Uh huh." The nervous Sugressa took a few steps away.

Fecanya looked back to the growling forest nymph. "How did you come to be named after a sauce, anyway?"

"Do you really want to discuss names?" Siraka asked.

Fecanya shrugged. "Fairy names tend to be uninspiring. I thought nymphs were more creative, though. Like, Galadriel, Milimania,

Poledancer, or Oaksap, or something." She tapped a finger to her lips. "How do you seduce a human with a name like Sriracha, or Oaksap?"

One of Siraka's vines elongated from her body, shooting straight for Fecanya.

Garbita sent a blast of magic at the nymph's back, but Siraka turned and deflected the assault.

Fecanya ducked under the stabbing vines and waggled her fingers toward Siraka just as she turned back. A cloud of blue sparkles materialized into a fist. The blue sparkly fist flew straight for the nymph, who leaned out of the way. The fist missed, but Fecanya pressed her thumb and forefinger together and twitched her hand left.

The fist redirected and turned into tiny blue particles which drifted up Siraka's nose.

"You," *sniff*, "are gonna pay for," *sniff*. Siraka's top lip twitched violently under her wrinkling nose. "Hufphtheuw!" Her green hair leaped over her head and fell in front of her face. She leaned back, mouth agape, and sneezed again, and again, her body jerking back and forth as though rowing a boat standing up.

Fecanya reached out her awareness into the forest. She found the hardened, pellet-like signature of a deer gone walkabout.

Siraka growled, head jerking sideways under the painful deer-turd assault. Her growl turned into a scream when an empty metal container filled with moldy fries smacked her in the side of the face.

Garbita waved her wand, and the mildewed missiles sped straight for the nymph's mouth. Unfortunately for Siraka, who'd been gritting her teeth through the hail of deer bullets, the fuzzy green and blue fries smashed into her teeth, turning her snarl the same color.

Siraka's enraged wail rumbled from her throat like an angry ibex. The nymph's wide eyes glowed green—matching her mold-coated teeth—and she flexed her fingers and straightened her arms toward the ground.

The forest trembled, and poison ivy vines sprouted from everywhere. The vines flowed all about the fairies, like writhing tentacles.

"This is not how civilized fey are supposed to behave!" Sugressa shouted over the cacophony of angry magic. She ducked under a vine that would have smacked her in the side of the face. Her wings beat furiously as she dodged in and out of the mass of swinging and stabbing plant limbs.

Fecanya waved her hands at a cluster of vines slithering toward her. She waggled her fingers, and several limbs wrapped around each other into a knot. "Do you actually have control over these things or are you just winging it?"

"You'll find out soon enough, fecal fairy, when I shove them down your throat."

"That's not very nice." Fecanya dodged another cluster of vines and noticed several dried cow patties lying on the wooded floor. With a wave and an upward swipe of her hand, the hardened manure missiles lifted into the air and spun toward the nymph.

Fecanya snapped her fingers just as Siraka blasted apart the spinning cow patties. "Wait! I *knew* that name sounded familiar." She zipped in and out of the gauntlet of vines, dipping low, then arcing up to stop right in front of Siraka's face.

"I remember seeing you in Mrs. Melgahind's garden, three years ago."

Siraka's eyes—and green snarl—widened. She lurched forward and tried to grab Fecanya, but she easily avoided the dryad's grasp. "Oh yes, I know who you are. Forest nymph?" Fecanya sniggered. "What? They have a nymph organization that provides promotions? Last I saw, you were—"

"Shut up!" Siraka leapt after Fecanya, hands outstretched. Bloomara sent a cloud of pollen into her face that sent her into another fit of sneezing.

"Hey girls!" Hovering out of reach, Fecanya flicked a smug grin down at Siraka before returning her attention to her companions. "Like I was saying, last I heard, she wasn't a forest nymph, but a *garden* nymph."

The other three fairies bobbed up and down as they hovered silently around the shaking Siraka.

Bloomara blinked.

Sugressa offered a hesitant but encouraging shrug.

Somewhere high up in a patch of trees, a pack of newly emigrated sugar gliders tittered.

"A what?" Garbita drifted around to hover beside the growling garden nymph. "How?" She looked Siraka up and down. "*How* can you be a garden *anything*? You're too large?"

Siraka slowly turned her baleful glare on Garbita. "For a magical being, you have a severe lack of imagination. I can shrink my size, you idiot! And I only did that gig while I was working on my skills for the forest—"

"Oooh, what're the gnomes like?" Sugressa zipped around to float in front of Siraka. "As odd as it sounds, I've only ever met one actual garden gnome in my life, but he was rather grumpy." Sugressa pressed her fists under her wide smile and glowing, gleeful orange eyes. "I imagine they're not all like that!"

"We've got plenty of gnomes at FWMS," Fecanya said dryly.

Sugressa half-turned to Fecanya. "Yes, but they're not garden gnomes," Sugressa said.

Siraka's mouth worked silently. "Some ... some're nice, I guess. Some're not. Just like anyone else. They do have this odd obsession with deep-fried radishes and kale ..." she trailed off, then blinked at Sugressa. "Are you mocking me?"

Sugressa gasped. "Why, no. I would never—"

"You think you're funny, don't you?" Her green hair floated about her head despite the lack of a breeze. "You all think I'm some kind of joke, don't you?"

"Now, now," Bloomara patted the air. "Calm yourself Miss Srira ..." she glared at Fecanya and cleared her throat, "Miss Siraka. No one is mocking anyone."

Siraka turned her suspicious gaze from one fairy to the next, meeting Fecanya, Bloomara, and Garbita's neutral gazes, and Sugressa's exaggerated smile. She gave a subtle shake of her head as she looked at the latter, then visibly relaxed.

In the loaded silence, Fecanya cleared her throat. "Well, on the bright side, at least your teeth match their little beards, now."

Siraka's nostrils flared. Vines whipped in every direction. The world went dark.

THIRTEEN

Fecanya woke to find herself pinned against a tree with a throbbing headache and a horrible itch exactly in the center of her back. "Ugh." Her head lolled to the side. She squirmed in an attempt to scratch her back, blinking away the blurriness in her vision. "I can feel my pulse in my head."

"Too *bad* you couldn't feel a proper *thought* in that cavernous place," she heard Garbita growl from somewhere below. "Per*haps* we could have come to an *amicable conclusion* to that conflict."

Fecanya strained to look down. Far below on the forest floor, Garbita waved her wand over a cluster of vines pinning her to the ground. The vines grudgingly slithered away. "I *swear*. Do you ever *think* before you *speak*?"

Fecanya waggled her fingers at the vines restraining her and they, too, withdrew. "Of course I do," she said, forcing her bruised wings to flutter before she fell. "It's kinda the only way to talk, isn't it?"

"You're a right foul git, Fecanya," Garbita said, picking herself up off the ground.

"What were you thinking?" demanded Bloomara's muffled voice.

Fecanya looked in the direction of the bloom fairy's voice and saw her pinned to a tree by just a single vine—or rather—a large leaf attached to the vine that wrapped around her head. Her wand appeared in her hand, and she angrily waved it over the vine.

"That really hurt," Sugressa said. "You made her super mad, Fecanya."

"Not everybody can sweet-talk everybody, Cloy," Fecanya replied.

"Maybe just try, one day," Sugressa suggested.

Fecanya rotated midair as she struggled to scratch the itch in the center of her back. "How is poison ivy affecting me? We're supposed to be immune."

"Against normal poison ivy, yes." Bloomara grimaced and scratched savagely at her underarms. "And thank you, Fecanya, for angering our quarry. We must now search her out. Again."

"Well, to be fair, Bloomara, I don't think she would have come along with us." Sugressa finally managed to extricate herself from a dog pile of leaves and vines, and began wiping her dress with her hands. She started to smile, but upon seeing Bloomara's glower, it came out as a nervous twitch.

"We've no time for arguments," Bloomara said. She pointed south. "The last thing I saw before one of those blasted vines smacked me in the mouth was her headed toward Seattle."

"Psst. Hey, buddy." Marvin adjusted his pleather, ankle-length trench and pulled his hat down further. He stuck his hands in his pockets as he strode closer to the woman sagging against the wall of the local Dollar Deals store. "Psst. Psssst. *PSSSSSSSSSSSSST!*"

The woman lifted her dim-eyed gaze to meet his. The flickering light in her forlorn gaze went from his eyes to his pockets. She pressed the butt of her hand against her forehead and winced. "What? What do you want? I don't have any—"

"I got some grounds, yo." He took a quick glance around, then lowered his voice as he leaned forward. "*Coffee* grounds, yo." He pulled his hand out just enough to reveal a plastic resealable sandwich bag half full of coffee grounds. He glanced down at the bag, then shrugged apologetically. "I know the bag ain't compostable. S'all I got, you understand."

The woman's eyes lit up. "How'd you get that? How much—"

Marvin frantically looked around while he patted the air between them. "Sssssh. Keep it down. You wanna get us jumped? Look ..." he stole another wary glance at their surroundings. "What you got?"

The woman reached into her pocket and pulled out a hundred-dollar bill. "I got this." She pointed at the packet containing the coffee grounds. "Give it to me."

Marvin snarled at her. "Look. Don't play with me, lady. You want these grounds, gimme a serious offer." He grinned at her. "A *real* offer."

The woman visibly shrank away. "No."

Marvin shrugged again and turned away to hide licking his lips. "Fine." He started to walk away.

"Wait, WAIT."

He turned back to see her reaching for him.

"Wait." She sighed. "Whatever you want."

"You know what I want."

She swallowed and reached down her shirt to produce an even smaller green bag, clearly compostable. She jerked her chin at his pocket. "How do I know that's the real stuff?"

"How do I know *that's* the real stuff?" Marvin asked, mimicking her gesture.

The woman's eyes flicked down at his pocket again, where his now sweating hand clasped the coffee ground baggie.

Marvin eyed the green bag in her hand. He folded his lips and licked them, but forced himself to wait.

"Guess we'll have to trust each other," she finally said.

They inched closer to one another, both reaching holding out their respective bags. Finally within reach, they snatched the bags from each other and backpedaled.

Marvin opened the stretchy green bag, closed his eyes, and inhaled deeply. When he opened his eyes again, he saw the woman had done the same. When she noticed him, she frowned. "Sugar don't have no smell, you know."

He shoved the bag in his pocket and lowered the brim of his hat just a little more to recover what was left of his noir. "Sentiment. It's the sentiment." His pleather coat squeaked as he shrugged once more and turned on his heel.

"You gonna be around tomorrow?" the woman called out from behind.

Coat flapping behind him in slow motion, Marvin stopped and half-turned to look back. "Could be. Could be not." With the most charismatic grin he could muster, Marvin started walking again. He turned forward just in time to see the nearby dumpster just as his face met it.

Marvin ignored the sound of a throat clearing behind him, straightened the now crinkled brim of his hat, and kept walking.

Fecanya whistled through her teeth. "This is bad."

"It will get a lot worse," Bloomara said. "How is sugar in short supply?"

Sugressa shrugged. "I make things sweeter, but I don't actually make sugar, Bloomara."

Fecanya stared at the head fairy. "How can you even ask that? You don't create flowers." She pointed at Garbita. "She doesn't create garbage, and I don't create sh—"

"Yes fine, FINE. My mistake." Bloomara waved her hand irritably. "Let's just move on."

The fairies glided on the winds at a safe distance overhead. They passed several human towns on their way to Seattle, all having descended into chaos.

"What's that horrible sound?" Sugressa said. She pointed at a cluster of houses. "It sounds like someone is torturing a human computer."

Fecanya nodded. "That's actually a good description. When they first created that network thing, their computers used to sound like that when they connected to it. I imagine it had to be painful."

"It's painful to me," Sugressa said, holding her hands to her pointed ears.

They collectively looked off to the side at the sound of a man shouting, "do you HAVE to do that now?"

"How dreadful." Garbita shook her head. "I can hear that man's telephone conversation from here."

Fecanya couldn't disagree. Even from their position, high in the air, she could hear the tiny voice coming through a man's phone.

"Nobody wants to know about you using Magenta Cycle to wash your underwear, buddy!"

"Then stop listening to my conversation," the phone man snapped back.

"How can I, when it's blasting through that stupid speaker on it?"

"That's the only way calls work on it, right now, okay?"

Fecanya giggled.

Bloomara pointed further down the street. "There's another one."

Then, Garbita pointed. "Over there, too."

All Fecanya could say was, "wow" as they glided overhead to the agonized screeching of computers dialing up to the internet, phone calls only working on speakerphone, and caffeine and sugar-deficient humans taking to the streets to damage one another.

"This is terrible," Sugressa said as a fight broke out over the last nectarine tart in a burgled bakery. "It feels like the apocalypse is coming. All that's left is for the Horsemen to arrive."

"Stop *being* so *dramatic*," Garbita said. "It's just *Washington*, Sugressa. The *Horsemen* are more likely getting *drunk* in a bar on another *world*, than facilitating an *apocalypse* here."

"But they're fighting," Sugressa said. "Look at them. They're fighting!"

Fecanya spared her a glance. "How much time have you ever spent around humans, Cloy?"

"Oh, Fecanya. Must you call me that?" Sugressa shrugged. "I dunno. I see them all the time."

"You *see* them during times when they're *consuming* something *sweet*, girl." Garbita waved a dismissive hand. "They're always *happy* when eating sweets."

"That's a great thing, Garbita," Sugressa said.

Fecanya sighed. "You ever been around humans when they're not consuming sweets or caffeine?"

Sugressa pressed a finger to her cheek and frowned. "Um. No."

Fecanya indicated the steadily budding riot. A man leapt atop a garbage bin and hefted a huge gun.

"Oh no!" Sugressa clamped her hands over her mouth. "He's going to shoot all those people!"

The man screamed and opened fire on the ground. Hundreds of green projectiles zipped into the mass of battling bodies.

"What ... what are those?" Garbita asked, wand half-raised over her head.

Bloomara squinted. "I believe those are ... brussels sprouts."

Fecanya frowned. "What? Why would he shoot them with brussels sprouts?"

"Have you ever touched a raw brussels sprout?" Bloomara asked.

Fecanya looked back to chaos. Humans ran in wide-eyed terror as the green mini-cabbage missiles whizzed into them. Those that weren't hit slipped on the rapidly spreading leaves coating the ground.

Sugressa flinched when a round of sprouts exploded into the back of a woman's head, and the shrapnel flew into the mouth of a hollering man beside her.

Fecanya cupped her hand over her mouth and nose as the distinct odor of raw brussels sprouts rose above the chaos to reach them. "I think we should get out of here."

"We can't leave them like that," Sugressa said.

Fecanya almost choked on her own guffaw. "Feel free to go down there and help."

"There's no use getting yourself *embroiled* in such an *omnishambles*, girl," Garbita said, grabbing her arm. "Come along."

"Wait." Bloomara pointed at a path glowing from pink to blue to orange, leading out of town. "Look."

Fecanya looked in the direction Bloomara pointed. "Fairy dust. Looks like someone left us a trail."

They magicked themselves invisible and angled down to get a closer look. A dark brown trail of sparkling dust floated in the air, snaking its way down the street and around the corner.

Sugressa sniffed, and her eyes popped open wide. "Woah. That's strong."

"Caffeinisa," Garbita said. "She left us a trail to follow."

"And one to keep us very awake while we do," Fecanya said, wiping her watering eyes.

"It won't do you any good."

They turned in the direction of the voice to see a fairy dressed in a bright green leaf dress, sitting against the wall and holding a cold press to the back of her head.

"Oh, goodness." Sugressa hurried over to the injured fairy. "Are you okay?"

The downed fairy slowly looked up at her. "Dandy."

"What happened?" Bloomara asked.

"I'm assuming you're looking for that wretch of a nymph who passed through here, recently. She whomped me on the back of the head real good. Threw me in a sack."

"And, you escaped?" Bloomara surmised.

"Nope. She realized I'm a vegetable fairy."

Everyone shared a collective "aaah."

"Ya," the fairy said. "It's not like humans are going to fight over something *healthy*, Lilith forbid."

"You're ..." Fecanya tapped her cheek. "You're Vegetina, right?"

Vegetina gingerly removed the cold press from her head and looked up. "At your service."

FOURTEEN

The glittering trail of fairy dust wove through the woods in a seemingly random fashion, yet no matter how far in any direction the path snaked, it always continued south.

"I'm starting to *wonder* if that nymph is *inebriated*," Garbita complained from the front of the procession.

Beside her, Bloomara huffed. "Likely, she's hunting for more prey to stuff in her sack on her way to Lilith knows where."

"She's slowing us down," Vegetina growled from the middle of the group. "She's on foot, we're flying. She can easily dart around in these woods while we have to change direction midflight. If she ran in a straight line, we'd catch up to her fast."

Vegetina looked over her shoulder at Fecanya and Sugressa, who brought up the rear. "When we catch up with that nymph I'm gonna make her eat those vines she wears. All of them."

Sugressa tilted her head and frowned. "Does anyone hear that?"

"Hear what?" Fecanya asked. She looked about the surrounding woods. Oaks, evergreens, and redwood trees all stared back at her, like faceless sentinels. Bird chatter filled in the silence while a gang of cicadas attempted to out-shout them. Somewhere in the brush, a wild turkey yelped authoritatively, and received loud sniggering from the local crows.

"A buzzing sound," Sugressa said. "It sounds like a bunch of bird-sized bugs buzzing ... that way." She pointed toward a town at the edge of the woods.

"We're looking for the nymph, Sugressa," Bloomara said. "Not—"

"Wait, I hear it, too," Fecanya said. "It's loud, Bloom. Sounds like a lot of them."

"Oh, that," Vegetina said. "It's the drones." At the other fairies' questioning look, she started in the direction Sugressa had indicated. "C'mon. I'll have to show you."

The buzzing grew so loud as they approached the edge of the woods that they had to clamp their hands over their ears.

"What in Lilith's bloody underworld *is* this racket?" Garbita yelled.

"Told you," Vegetina shouted back. "Drones!"

She pointed higher in the sky, where dozens of drones hovered in the air, their tiny propellers whirling to keep them airborne.

Sugressa pointed at a nearby drone with a medium-sized package clutched in its metal spider legs. "Is that thing holding a box?"

Fecanya sighed, though she couldn't hear it over the maddening buzz of the drones. "They're drones from that human store, Nile dot com. I've heard about them. Humans use their interweb thingie on their computers to get packages sent to their homes."

"But these aren't delivering," Sugressa said. "They're just sitting there. Well, so to speak."

"It's their interwebs," Vegetina said. "When the nymph found a way to break their interwebs, it threw everything haywire. She was smart, though." Vegetina waved a hand at the drones. "She didn't totally break it. The humans would have been forced to accept that. No, she broke it just enough that it only works with their old mortars they hook up to."

"You mean modems?" Fecanya replied, then she remembered the agonized wailing of hundreds of computers trying to dial into the interwebs in the last town they'd visited. "Why didn't I think of that before?" She pulled out her smartphone.

Garbita hissed. "Put that contraption *away*, Fecanya! I can't *believe* you're still *using* that thing."

Fecanya scrolled through the tiny icons on her screen, then tapped the one she was looking for.

"How is your phone still working?" Sugressa asked. "All the human phones seem to be down or not working right."

Fecanya bit back a sarcastic reply. "It's not like I'm going to a service and paying them with their paper sheets, Sugressa. The phone acts like a focus. Ah! There it is."

The fairies gathered around.

Garbita's lips screwed up as if she'd tasted something dreadful. "Feybook?"

"Yup," Fecanya replied. "Easy way to keep in touch across long distances. More instant than magicking up a conference cloud."

She scrolled through endless threads regarding the recent events. A thread featuring videos of humans fighting in the streets and titled "Primates Gone Wild" was trending.

Another news thread started by Caffeine Fairies United displayed video footage of human law enforcement standing guard against desperate mobs of humans grappling outside the doors of Galaxydoe coffee shops.

"Oh my goodness." Sugressa held a hand over her mouth. "So many fighting. This is so sad."

"Speak for yourself," Fecanya said. She pointed at a photo of a woman slapping a man in the side of the head with a bag of flour. The caption read "When Sugar Scams Go Wrong."

"Oh my," Bloomara said. "This is quite ... quite fascinating. You just touch the ..." She touched the screen of a news video.

"... global phenomenon, Larry," a reporter said. "There are reports coming in of coffee bean shortages across the state and possibly farther reaching across the country. While factories assure coffee sellers that the beans are being picked like normal, they're arriving at coffee shops decaffeinated.

"Reports are also coming in of problems with the internet. Only first-generation dialup modems are functional but not consistently reliable. Clean-up crews have been working around the clock, cleaning up the debris of discarded computers. John Jackleson is on location in Everett. On to you, John."

A sandy blond-haired John Jackleson with five o'clock shadows and dark rings under his eyes stared blankly at the camera during the broadcast delay.

"Thanks, Jill. Things have been tense with so many anomalies happening seemingly all at once. I've got Mr. Warblson here with me from Waste Cleanup Management." He turned to Mr. Warblson and held the microphone out. "Mr. Warblson, how has this affected you and your colleagues."

A rather tall man, Mr. Warblson had to fold himself nearly in half to get his head in frame with the news anchor. His sun-browned bald head was creased with stress lines that could rival a map. "Well I ..." He grunted and grabbed the mic from the news anchor, his meaty fist swallowing all but the black foam bubble at the top.

"Look here, folks. I'm gonna say this really careful for ya. Stop. Chuckin'. Your. Computers. Look here. I know it's frustrating that it's taking you five minutes per website to surf the web, but that ain't ground for—"

A loud crash sounded just off camera. The top of John Jackleson's head disappeared from the camera, along with his hands, that went in and then out of frame as he ducked.

Mr. Warblson chuckled as he reached down and grabbed Jackleson by the back of his suit jacket and lifted him back into frame. "You see here?" He looked to Mr. Jackleson and gave him a sympathetic shake for the camera's sake. "Another one of those blasted computers some nitwit chucked out of a five-story building! Stop. Chuckin'. Your. Computers!"

He pointed into the camera with a thick, leathery finger that looked to have more muscles in it than Jackleson's entire body. "Don't make me come for you! Cuz I will. I swear it. I'll come find you chuckin' your computers and I'll strangle—"

The camera cut back to the studio where the news anchor cleared her throat. To the left, her colleague put a fist to his mouth and coughed.

"Well, then. Reports are coming in from all over Washington of the caffeine shortage, Nile dot com drones hovering over every metropolitan area, waiting for a delivery order, and sugar shortages are causing bakeries across the state to use stevia. Law enforcement is advising citizens to stay home if you can—"

Fecanya turned off the video and whistled through her teeth.

"How positively dreadful," Garbita said.

"And it'll get much worse if we don't find that nymph," Bloomara said.

Fecanya stuffed the phone back into her extra-dimensional sack. Something still nagged at her. There wasn't anything inherently odd about a nymph causing mischief. Sure, they might occasionally lure a human into a tree and leave them stuck there for hours. She'd even seen one trick a human into wrapping themselves into a woven blanket of poison ivy. She might have even laughed.

"Our errand has become even more urgent," Bloomara declared. "We must find the nymph before she can inflict any more anarchy."

They returned to the trail of fairy dust, leaving the paralyzed drones hovering in the air, waiting on destinations for their packages.

Fecanya absently followed. Something about this wasn't right, and at the same time, felt familiar. She'd never heard of a nymph going to this much trouble for any reason, let alone to toy with humans. Bloomara and Garbita's conversation gradually faded as Fecanya pondered the situation. Then, she heard a sound that sent a shiver down her spine.

Disembodied giggling.

FIFTEEN

Vegetables large and small zipped through the air. Mud balls pounded into the heads and backs of unfortunate recipients. A bowl of over-cooked spaghetti smashed into the side Jimmy's Surf Turf and Macaroons pub. From every direction, humans gradually descending into madness assaulted each other with anything within reach.

"Oh. Dear. Me."

Fecanya glanced at Garbita's ashen face. "You ok?"

"Dear, dear me," Garbita echoed as though she hadn't heard. "They're going to destroy everything. They're going to wreck everything."

Fecanya looked back out, just beyond the edge of the woods where they hid. Humans. Everywhere.

"I hope they don't hurt themselves," Sugressa said.

"To Lilith's underworld with *them*," Garbita said. "There will be rubbish *everywhere*. The *streets* are already *filling* with it. If this keeps up, we could call in Detritus Redistributors from across the country and it would *still* take days to clean it all up!"

Vegetina looked at the chaotic scene below with an air of indifference. "From childhood to adulthood, their health experts tell 'em "less sugar, more vegetables", but they never listen."

She glanced at Sugressa's crestfallen expression and gave her a pat on the shoulder. "That wasn't aimed at you, Sweets. I'm talking about that stuff they make in their factories." She looked back. "If they ate more vegetables and less deep-frying them in those lard sandwiches, they might—"

"What?" Garbita interrupted. "Lard *what?*"

"Oh, you heard me," Vegetina replied. "Most of the vegetables these humans eat are smothered in some sort of sauce or gravy, deep-fried, the works. The latest trend is slicing deep-fried vegetables up and putting them in lard sandwiches."

All the color drained from Sugressa's face. "I'll be right back."

"I feel nauseous just saying this," Fecanya said. "But, I agree with Garbita. If we don't find that nymph and set this right, they're going to wreck everything and we'll end up on cleaning duty."

The fairies magicked themselves invisible and zipped out of the trees, giving the crazed populace a wide berth.

"My goodness me," Garbita breathed. "They're positively foaming at the mouth."

They flew around the back of a restaurant when they heard Sugressa call out from behind.

"Hey, don't leave me!"

Fecanya turned and gasped. Sugressa sped right through the middle of a clump of humans wrestling over a large sack of coffee grounds.

The sound of ripping burlap drowned out the shouting and punching just as Sugressa flew between the embattled humans.

Fecanya cringed. "Uh oh."

Time is known for having a rather practical sense of humor that few appreciate. It cannot stop or reverse itself, but it does have a few tricks up its sleeve. One such trick is speed. This is why weekends tend to bobsled back to the workweek, and napping while the infant is asleep seems to end, the instant an overtired parent closes their eyes.

Conversely, it has created many a moment where a glass filled with an un-cleanable beverage drops slowly from a counter to the carpeted floor, while helpless onlookers watch in expletive-ridden resolve despite being mere inches from the glass.

This was Time's moment to shine.

Fecanya could only watch as tiny threads in the sack frayed and snapped, holding together just long enough for the oblivious Sugressa to pass nearby.

"Let go and gimme the sack!" the wild-eyed woman said. "It's mine, I told ya."

"Yeh can't make meh!" the man on the other end of the sack shouted. He wiped a bit of froth from the corner of his mouth. "Yeh can't make meh!"

Curses filled the air and were quickly drowned out by the coffee sack finally giving up.

Sugressa went down in an airborne tsunami of coffee grounds.

"Oh my goodness," Bloomara wailed. "NO!"

"Sugressa!" Fecanya shouted.

The coffee grounds washed Sugressa onto the sidewalk like waves from the ocean depositing her onto the beach.

Fecanya was the first to reach her. She turned Sugressa onto her side and gave her back a slap. The sugar fairy convulsed and coughed up a cloud of coffee dust. The creases on Fecanya's forehead deepened as she looked Sugressa over. "You're gonna be okay." She wiped coffee grounds off of Sugressa's face and looked to the others. "Help me get her off the sidewalk before we all get trampled."

They carried Sugressa around the corner and into an alley behind a strip of stores.

"You're gonna be okay," Fecanya repeated as they gingerly lay her onto the concrete. "Just take it easy." Without taking her eyes off Sugressa, she snapper her fingers and a pitcher of water appeared in the air.

"Here." Fecanya gingerly lifted Sugressa's head and helped her sip.

A series of loud growls came from around the corner, followed by a heavy thud and a high-pitched whimper.

Everyone shared a nervous glance.

"What was that?" Bloomara asked.

Vegetina peeked around the corner and whistled through her teeth. "Good call getting her outta there. A woman just dove into the pile of coffee grounds." She flinched. "Oooh. The man grabbed her by the ankle to pull her out, and she head-butted him in the crotch."

"Sugressa." Fecanya tossed the pitcher into the air and it disappeared with a 'poof'. She gave Sugressa's shoulder a gentle squeeze. "Hey. You okay?"

"Mrgph." With an effort, Sugressa lifted herself up to her elbows. She noted Fecanya's helping hand and smiled, coffee grounds sliding out of her hair down her face. "Were you worried about me?"

Fecanya snorted. "Hardly. I just didn't want to carry you the rest of the—"

"You were worried about me, weren't you? You were!"

"Will you keep it down," Fecanya hissed. "Those primates will hear ..." she trailed off and looked into Sugressa's dilated pupils. "Hey. You okay?"

Sugressa responded with an exaggerated nod, more coffee grounds flying. "M'great! Great!"

She pointed down the alley. "Aren't we supposed to hunt down a nymph?" She looked at Garbita. "Which way were we going?" She looked down the other end of the alley. "Did you hear that? Someone got punched in the knees! What was that sound?" Sugressa rose into the air. "We gotta hurry and catch that nymph!"

The over-caffeinated sugar fairy zipped up and down the alley in every direction, then flew off into the distance.

Sixteen

Vegetina seemed to realize her mouth was hanging open and shut it. "Um ... wow."

"We don't have time for this," Bloomara said. "Every moment we tarry here, the nymph gets farther away."

"Let's split up," Fecanya suggested. "You and Garbita can keep tracking the nymph and Vegetina and I can go after Sugressa."

Vegetina frowned. "I want to be there to punch that nymph's lights out when we find her."

"Don't you worry," Fecanya said. "Considering the whammy she put on us the last time we met, those two aren't doing anything rash till we catch up."

Garbita crossed her arms in indignation but didn't dispute the reasoning.

"Hey, Bloom." Fecanya pointed in the direction Sugressa had gone. After we find her, the trail might have faded too much to see—"

"We will leave you a fresh trail of sparkles, Fecanya. Just ..." Bloomara chewed her bottom lip. "Just be careful. There's no telling what trouble Sugressa may have gotten into, and the humans have gone rabid."

The bloom fairy's uncharacteristic concern caught Fecanya so off guard that she refrained from teasing her about it. "Um yeah. Thanks, um." She waved an uncomfortable hand in Bloomara and Garbita's direction. "Yeah um you two be careful, too. Wouldn't want to step into a bear trap or get head-butted by a bison or anything."

Fecanya took off, and moments later Vegetina caught up. "That was ... abrupt," the vegetable fairy remarked. "It was also the most uncomfortable kindness I've ever seen shared between two parties."

"Yeah we're complicated like that," Fecanya said. "They find me annoying and I find them nauseating."

"Or, you're closer friends than any of you want to admit, because your personalities are so different."

Fecanya gave her a sidelong glance. "Feels like you're a secret agent sent by my therapist."

Vegetina shrugged. "I call it like I see it." She jerked her chin ahead. "What's their problem?"

They glided to a stop and hovered above a crowd of ants encircling a loaf of partially eaten rye bread. "Ugh. I'll never do that again," one ant said. It lay on its back with its middle legs rubbing its swollen abdomen. "That was way too much."

"Blergh," another ant groaned. "I thought sweetened rye bread would be a treat." It shuffled to one side and fell over. "S'like somebody smothered that loaf in a gravy made of sugar. I hope it doesn't give me the diabetus."

"She's definitely been this way," Fecanya said.

They magicked themselves invisible and flew out of the alley. The aftermath of Sugressa's passing was immediately apparent. They glided past Yamen's Ramen, where patrons explained to a mortified cook that their ramen dishes tasted like candied licorice.

A taco stand further down the street struggled to keep up with the overflowing demand for their suddenly sweet combo taco platters.

Vegetina wrinkled her nose. "Who could eat a sweet taco?"

"It's tacos," Fecanya replied. "Something about them drives humans to the point of insanity. You could throw a taco in the middle of a cage and they'd trap themselves in it if it meant they get to eat tacos."

"This is *way* too much sugar, sir," a voice said from a patio just as Fecanya and Vegetina flew overhead. They looked at each other and stopped to listen.

The server frowned in confusion at the glucose quicksand slithering around the bottom of the patron's mug. "Apologies, sir, but I didn't add anything to it. The sugar packs are there." She pointed to a ceramic container sparsely populated by multicolored packets. "It's actually surprising that you got that much real sugar at all, sir," the server went on. "It's been a struggle to get the little bit we have. There's been a shortage of everything but Stevia ..."

"She's close by," Fecanya said. "That much fresh sugar means she isn't far away."

"I think we'd better hurry and find her before she sweetens half the human population in this town to death." Vegetina pointed at an open market pavilion. Humans milled about, shopping and consuming various drinks and food items.

The closer they drew to the market, the more Fecanya picked up bits of conversation from confused humans, wondering why their meal or drink was suddenly too sweet to consume.

And in the middle of the crowd hovered an invisible—to humans, anyway—Sugressa.

"*You* get a sweetie. And *you* get a sweetie. And *youuuuuu* get a sweetie!" She turned to see a woman sitting at a bench with a plate of steaming liver 'n' onions. She closed her eyes and inhaled the aroma, then sighed and lifted her fork and knife.

Sugressa screwed her face into an upside-down smile. "Poor human; having to eat such a dreadful dish. I'll help you enjoy it!"

Fairy sparkles settled over the dish, including the piece of impaled liver ascending toward the woman's mouth. Several masticating moments later, the woman leaned away from her plate.

"Looks like her whole face is trying to retreat from the bite she just took," Vegetina observed. She looked over at Sugressa, who darted in every direction, sweetening everything from the boiled eggs and hummus sandwich of one man, to the plantain and spinach burger of another. "I think she's gone crazy."

Fecanya watched Sugressa tirelessly zipping from place to place, sweetening everything she encountered, including a muddy cinderblock. *I've got to put a stop to this*, she thought. *Doggon Leowitriss. I think I'm gonna be sick.* She silently cursed the satyr therapist. It had to be his fault, for the longer Fecanya watched, the more she realized with growing discomfort that she considered Sugressa a friend. Not just any friend, but her *best* friend, and watching Sugressa now, Fecanya felt an even more uncomfortable feeling. Concern.

SEVENTEEN

"We'd better go get her now before she—" Fecanya began
            "Aaaaaand she's gone." Vegetina blinked. "That's impressive. I can barely keep up with her."

"Ya," Fecanya said as they took off after her. "And if we don't get her under control she's going to break the sound barrier."

They flew between oaks and evergreens. Following the sugar-laden sparkle trail, they zipped upward spiraling circles around moss-covered redwoods.

"I've seen ... patterns ... like this before," Vegetina huffed. "I had a job ... with a household ... where the parents ... had a fridge full ... of uneaten vegetables. As I flew past them ... to freshen up some withering kale bushels, I saw ... a toddler ... with crayons scribbling ... on paper. This looks ... like that."

"Better save your breath," Fecanya said. Having long been used to keeping up with Sugressa, she wasn't tired so much as her rapidly beating wings felt like they were generating enough heat to warm a house.

"Um, I think we're getting close again." Vegetina pointed at a swarm of bees hovering around a hive oozing honey into the gaping maw of a bliss-drunken black bear.

"They don't look happy," Fecanya said from the corner of her mouth.

She scanned the bulging hive that was practically hemorrhaging honey. "Yup. Sugressa's been here.

The bees spotted them. As one they formed up defensive ranks around the hive and glared at the two fairies

Fecanya and Vegetina held up their hands in a placating gesture. "Woah, now," Fecanya said. "We're just looking for a friend. "Maybe you've seen—"

A particularly large and unhappy bumble bee slowly lifted one of its legs and pointed southeast, never taking its eyes off of Fecanya's. It bent its leg, then jabbed it in that direction again.

"Well, uh, thanks. We'll just go—"

The bumble bee bent its leg, and jabbed it again.

The bees stared after them for a long time, then turned and did the equivalent of placing one's fists on their hips while surveying a well-done disaster. Fortunately everyone had evacuated in time before that insane sugar fairy zipped past and caused everything to overflow.

Down below, Nicholas, the local black bear now lay flat on his back with his maw open. If someone didn't stop him, the fool was going to drown himself.

They didn't find Sugressa, right away. Instead, they found a crowd of cheering squirrels encircling Sugressa and another squirrel. Furry rodent bodies bobbed in coordinated rhythm, tails twitching in sync as though to music only they could hear.

Vegetina snorted and cupped her hand over her grin. "Oh, this is rich."

Pink hair swished in and out of view over furry heads, followed by a set of sweeping ankles.

Fecanya and Vegetina rose higher for a better view.

Sugressa sprinted inside the circle's perimeter, then performed a two-handed, then no-handed cartwheel. She swept her arms back as she stomped a foot forward, then the other foot. She dropped her hands to the ground and soon her body was a veritable windmill, spinning and flipping, kicking up enough breeze to set the local leaves leaning away. She ended the dance with her knees tucked to her stomach, spinning on her back.

A winded squirrel watched in disbelief on the opposite side of the circle as Sugressa picked up speed.

There were high-pitched groans and cheers through the squirrel crowd, as acorns exchanged paws.

"Can't say I've ever seen anything like this, before," Vegetina said.

Sugressa sprang off her back and landed on one hand, still spinning.

"You hang around that one long enough, you'll see all sorts of things," Fecanya said. "We'd better go get her."

"When she's done," Vegetina said. "I'm not getting laid out in the middle of a bunch of kleptomaniac squirrels."

Finally, Sugressa slowed down enough to be seen by the naked eye again, and Fecanya and Vegetina rushed in.

Fecanya made an effort at a sheepish grin. "Sorry, everyone. Show's over."

They grabbed Sugressa under the arms and whisked her away into the trees. Angry chirping followed them through the branches. They reached an abandoned heron's nest and deposited the sugar fairy in the middle.

"Hold her down," Fecanya said.

"Easier said than done," Vegetina growled, barely able to hold the hyper fairy on her back. "I wouldn't mind if you hurry."

"C'mon!" Sugressa complained. "I was just getting started. I'vego-tadancetofinish and Ihavemoresugaringtodo!"

Fecanya magicked up a human-sized espresso mug full of chamomile tea, held Sugressa by the chin, and poured the tea into her mouth. That done, she helped Vegetina hold her down until Sugressa finally stopped struggling.

She blinked, then turned her bewildered expression on the other two. "F ... Fecanya?"

"It's me hyper-head," Fecanya said.

They released her and helped her sit up.

Sugressa held her hand to her head and winced. "What happened?"

"You got a face full of coffee and went insane," Fecanya said.

"Oh. Is that why my head hurts?"

"Either that or spinning on top of it," Vegetina said. "You're lucky we got to you before you burned in a bald spot."

"We need to get going," Fecanya said. "Bloom and Garbita continued on the nymph's trail."

"Oh no! We've got to get to them before the nymph does, Fecanya."

The trio took off, retracing their path until they reached the little town of now lethargic humans and found the nymph's trail once again.

Bloomara and Garbita followed the trail of fairy dust to the base of a gnarled oak. The old giant stood amidst pines, firs, and spruces, all leaning away as though they'd rather have stood anywhere else in the world.

"I don't like the look of those fellows." Garbita gestured toward a committee of vultures staring down at them with expressions that insinuated they were enjoying some private joke.

One of the vultures extended its wrinkled neck and grinned—insomuch as anything possessed of a beak can grin.

"Well then," Bloomara said. "I think we should enter sooner rather than later."

"Must I remind you the risks of entering a nymph's tree?" Garbita said from the corner of her mouth.

"What choice have we?" Bloomara replied. "We cannot wait for the others."

"Sure you can."

Bloomara hopped with a frightened yelp and turned on her heel to face the speaker.

"Ffffffffff!" Garbita whirled, brandishing her wand.

The nymph caught her wrist. She waggled her fingers, and vines sprang from the ground and bound both fairies' arms to their sides. The nymph winked a pale green eye.

EIGHTEEN

"... Across all of Seattle and its surrounding suburbs. Governor Hal Heckelsmith in a recent press conference has stated that he intends to deploy the national guard—"

"Oh no," Sugressa moaned. "Those poor humans. They're suffering."

Vegetina snorted back her bark of laughter, and Fecanya began to wonder if the vegetable fairy was her long lost sister.

"Suffering? Humans? Have you spent any time at all around them?" Vegetina pointed at the video playing on Fecanya's phone. "I spend a lot of time trying to make vegetables as attractive as possible so the primates will eat them and live longer."

She cupped her chin in her hand and frowned. "Though, now that I say it out loud, I don't know why I do it. I mean, it's my job and always has been, but ... why?" She gave her head a shake. "Anyway, I can tell you that humans are predisposed to problems and suffering. It's what they do. They've spent thousands of years perfecting it, and they've succeeded."

"It's true," Fecanya chimed in. "Early in my career I worked an extra shift to help out a hermit living in the mountains. He'd planted a garden but the soil wasn't fertile enough. I helped him out by transporting extra fertilizer a herd of bovines left, farther up the hill. Deposited the stuff and spread it across his garden overnight while he slept."

"What happened?" Sugressa asked, the apocalyptic video temporarily forgotten.

"The guy was happy for a while. Veggies grew nice and healthy. He raised a few chickens and a cow. Had eggs and milk, everything a human could need." She shrugged. "Lived comfortable and carefree for about a month."

Vegetina arched an eyebrow. "Let me guess. He became a B.E."

Fecanya snapped her fingers and pointed at Vegetina. "Precisely."

Sugressa looked from one to the other. "What's a B.E.?"

"Bored Exhibitionist," Fecanya explained. "When things get too peaceful and too quiet for humans, they get bored. Then, one of two things happen. They either start thinking a lot and depress themselves, or find creative ways to shorten their life expectancy.

"The hermit had plenty to eat, and lived in the fresh air, surrounded by nature and tranquility. So ..." She shrugged a shoulder. "He took up 'predator rumping'."

Both Sugressa and Vegetina looked at each other, then turned questioning expressions on Fecanya. "Predator what?"

"You heard me. Predator rumping. The farmer coined the term for himself. He would sneak up on apex predators from behind, slap them on the rump, then take off. Obviously the offended apex predator would give chase. The game was to get to safety before it caught him."

"That ... sounds," Vegetina shook her head. "How long did he play that game?"

"Till a grizzly bear caught him."

Sugressa gasped. "That's terrible!"

"Sure, terrible," Vegetina said. "How many grizzlies did he slap before one caught him?"

"Oh, the first one." Fecanya shrugged again. "I went and turned his chickens and cow loose. The cow filled up on what it could find on his land, then went and joined the other bovines up in the hills I told it about. The local Cervidae cruising the area took care of his garden."

"Fecanya!" Sugressa glared at her. "Why didn't you help him?"

"What would I have done, Cloy? Warned him? I'm sure he wouldn't have thought himself insane listening to a disembodied voice, and I certainly wasn't going to show myself to him and get shoved in a jar.

"Anyway. My point is, you can't stop humans from suffering. In fact, *not* suffering would cause them suffering." She tapped the sound icon on the news broadcast.

"... Royal Order of Disorganizationists have declared that it's time to announce their Religion of Disorganization. We have Philbert Robidaiah on location with a representative of this ... religion. Philbert?"

A man in cardboard-brown slacks, flannel shirt, and striped tie reaching to his sternum stood with his ear pointed toward the ground as though expecting the news anchor's voice to come from there.

"Thank you, Barbara. I'm standing here with a gentleman who calls himself The Messiah of Disorganization." His shirt sleeve retreated from his wrist to halfway up his forearm as he indicated the man next to him.

The Messiah of Disorganization ran a skeletal hand over the back of his head where the remainder of his green and orange dyed hair resided. He leaned in closer to Philbert, despite the former holding the mic out to him.

"We just wanna make it clear that all this," he flapped a hand to indicate the world around them, "organized nonsense ain't no good to nobody. You already see the signs! Houses 'n cars 'n stores 'n money. All of it's a farce. We ain't need none of that. A fella should be able to walk into any place and grab uh head uh lettuce! We should be able to take that slab o' ribs and chow down.

"Ain't nobody can tell me we need money 'n anti-theft ... stuff, to stop a man from livin'. That's alls we want. Just a chance to *live*!"

Philbert Robidaiah closed his hanging mouth. "I see. But, without organization and structure, how would there be stores for you to obtain products? How would there be any place for you to obtain those ribs to ... chow down on, sir?"

The Messiah bobbed his head and chewed the inside of his bottom lip through the whole question. "M'glad you asked that. The answer is folks. *Folks* is the answer. Folks takes care of folks! Without all this concrete and ... and ... chairs, and ... and buildings and cars, we'd be left back to folks! Somebody would make up a farm and grow them corns 'n cabbages 'n, 'n, 'n shrimps 'n tacos for us tuh eats. We just gots to let it happen oooooooh naturaaaaaaaale ..."

Back in the news studio, News Anchor Barbara watched Philbert watch The Messiah of Disorganization thrust his arms out wide, shredded jacket and matching tattered jeans flapping as though they'd narrowly survived the affections of a Bull Shark.

He turned in circles like an odoriferous windmill, chanting his "oh naturale" mantra as nearby followers took up the cadence.

"Uuh, there ... there you have it, Barbara. The Religion of Disorganization—"

An off-camera shout stopped Philbert short. The camera swung away to a mob of toga-clad men and women. The crowd of at least forty humans wore large soup rolls on their heads, creating the image of a cluster of brown-capped mushrooms.

A man stepped forward and puffed his chest out. As he spoke, little white flecks took flight from the depths of his cotton-like beard.

"Weeeee are the Glutenists!" he bellowed—or rather, tried to bellow, but his voice cracked. "We are the heralds of the Bread God, who shall return in this hour of need."

The Glutenists reached under their togas and drew forth two-foot-long baguettes. As though holding Olympic torches, the Glutenists marched forth, chanting about the second coming of the Bread God and the breaking of the chains of bread oppression.

"I think they've gone insane," Vegetina said. "I mean *really* insane."

"We need to find that nymph and get the caffeine back, for a start." Fecanya frowned at the screen. She didn't want to believe it. She wanted to think that she'd heard anything else but that disembodied giggling. She'd heard the same sound a year ago before they'd narrowly averted the tragedy of the wastewater plant. Imps. She shivered.

"You all right?" Vegetina asked.

"We *really* need to find that nymph. There's a lot more to this than coffee and human technology failure."

Vegetina waved a hand at Fecanya's phone.

Baguette spears held high, the Glutenists bleated a war cry and charged the Disorganizationists, much to the confusion of all; including the Disorganizationists.

NINETEEN

E ven under the best of circumstances, the natural and magical world viewed humans as a species that had snuggled up comfortably with its own lunacy long ago. These weren't the best of circumstances.

Forest animals retreated deeper into the woods, and even raccoons— the most "come at me bro" species aside from wolverines—decided enough was enough and fled back into the forest.

The fairies whizzed between trees, hiding behind mailboxes, inside bushes, and anywhere else that provided cover from the chaos.

"Why are we hiding?" Sugressa asked. "We're already invisible."

"They may be crazy," Fecanya said, "but even humans can sense when something's nearby, even if they can't see it. Wouldn't want to stray too close and catch an elbow in the face.

From overhead someone shouted about the ruckus down below, and out of the window flew an internet router. The tablet-sized device arced across the sky and began its descent straight for the two embattled factions.

It collided with the hardened sourdough helmet of a Glutenist. The electronic missile exploded in a shower of little plastic parts, yanking the bread helmet with it. Bits of organic and inorganic shrapnel showered the combatants, mixing together to deposit themselves into the gaping maws of the bellowing "soldiers."

"If we weren't trying to find that nymph and our friends," Vegetina said, "I'd stick around for the show—"

Fecanya swallowed. "Did you see that?"

Still coming down off of her caffeine high, Sugressa pressed her hand to the space just below her forehead. "Mmph. See what?"

"There. Look there!" Fecanya pointed out the dark silhouette of a bat-winged creature flapping beside the head of a woman. It used a tiny pitch-fork to lift the wheat soup bowl helmet and whisper into her ear. The woman's eyes narrowed, and she drew back and launched her baguette into the back of a Disorganizationist's head.

She ran screaming right behind the bread missile and jumped on the staggered man's back. She howled, snatched off her soup bowl roll helmet, and began beating the man over the head with it.

"That was an imp!" Fecanya hissed. "They're back."

"An imp?" Vegetina squinted at the scene. "Wait ... I think I remember something in the company communiqué about imps nearly destroying a bunch of wastewater plants in Arizona."

"Yup," Fecanya said.

"You were involved in that?"

"Garmon City would have taken the worst bath imaginable if we hadn't been there."

Vegetina turned her open-mouthed, upside-down smile toward the riot. "Are you telling me there's shit imps goading these humans to fight?"

"Well, they're not exactly shit imps, but they'd found a way to use ..." Fecanya shook her head. "Don't worry about the details. I'm pretty certain these are at least the same type of imp, and we need to keep them from fully materializing in this world."

A translucent imp jabbed a Glutenist in the rear end with its little pitchfork. The man howled and thrust his hips forward. This in itself wouldn't have been a bad thing, had his hips not been in such close prox-imity to a particularly muscular woman's posterior in front of him.

"Just what do you think you're doing, masher!" She grabbed the unfortunate man by the neck and began violently shaking him.

"I didn't know a human's arms and legs could wriggle like that," Sugressa said. "It's like he has no skeleton."

Disembodied giggling filled the air. Vegetina and Sugressa nervously scanned the area.

"That the laughing you were talking about?" Vegetina asked.

Fecanya nodded. "Looks like they found another way to enter this dimension. Chaos. Must not be enough yet, but if they can affect humans in this way, they're close."

"Um." Sugressa pointed. "I think it must be enough, Fecanya." She pointed to a cluster of tiny portals opening in the air. A swarm of bat-winged imps poured out of the portal, pitchforks in hand, and wolf muzzle grins glinting with delight.

The three fairies huddled closer into the thickest part of the bush.

"We need to get out of here and find the others so we can figure out how to stop this," Fecanya whispered. "Just a small batch of the little bastards are enough to send this little town into chaos."

"Do you think they'll recognize us?" Sugressa asked.

"Probably," Fecanya said. "Just keep a low profile and try not to get spotted—"

"Hey!" a tiny voice squeaked. "I know you!"

Fecanya swore under her breath.

"Hey! Brimbibor!" An imp with a furry mohawk pointed at them while waving over his shoulder at a companion." It's that fairy. The one who put the whammy on us last year! The one who collects shit!"

"I do not *collect* shit, you idiot." Fecanya buzzed right up to the imp and punched him in the face.

"Ow!" The imp covered his face with his hands. "You broke my nose!"

"Tell me who's spreading rumors that I collect shit, or I'll break more than that."

"Brimbibor. Get her."

Roughly a foot tall—twice the height of a normal imp—the hulking Brimbibor was armed with a blood-red trident practically dripping with dark magic. He grinned, displaying a mouthful of sharp teeth, and narrowed his glowing green eyes.

"Fecanya?" Sugressa's voice called softly behind her. "I think we should probably go."

Brimbibor glanced past her at Sugressa, then returned his malevolent gaze to Fecanya's. He flexed his furry chest, covered in corded muscles, and hefted the trident, providing a clear view of his heavily muscled arms. His gleaming smile brightened.

Fecanya had to clamp her eyes shut for a moment, not because of the brightness of Brimbibor's smile, but to keep from being dizzied by said smile as it bounced erratically in the air as the burly imp flapped toward her with the grace of an inebriated bat.

TWENTY

Vegetina cast the approaching imp a doubtful look. "I don't know whether to laugh or flee."

"He looks dangerous," Sugressa said.

"Ya, if he can get his hands on you, but it looks like he can barely fly. How do imps get anywhere with that clumsy flight?"

"Like this," a squeaky voice said.

Vegetina turned to see the imp that had recognized them, having somehow gotten at their back. His tail curled, arrowhead pointed at Vegetina like a coiled snake ready to strike. And strike, it did.

"Ow!" Vegetina rubbed her arm and glared at the imp.

"Heheheh. Our venom is deadly. You've only got a few moments left—"

Vegetina slapped the imp across the face. When the unfortunate creature stopped spinning, she slapped it on top of its bald head.

The force of the slap drove the imp's chin down into its chest forcing its shoulders upward into an awkward shrug.

"Grgh!"

If the imp had been able to think past the current moment of pain and bewilderment, he might have wondered why the poison hadn't worked.

Imps and fairies are related only in that they are both sprites, but the similarity tends to end there. Fairies being—generally—a kindly species that also do things like research, understand that the fey species is immune to poison, both earthly and abysmal.

Unfortunately for this soon-to-be-battered imp, his species did not, in fact, have access to such things as books and shared knowledge. In the devil world, you tended to just wing it and see how things turned out. Sometimes things turned out badly.

"How dare you stab me with that oily tail of yours, you crusty rodent!" Vegetina growled.

"They can teleport short distances," Fecanya said as Vegetina grabbed a tuft of the whimpering imp's chest fur and began shaking him. "If we can get enough distance between us and them, we can get away."

"I think she's going to beat that imp up some more," Sugressa said.

Brimbibor was nearly on top of them by then. "Gungus sackinmondo morgish flourshen."

Sugressa's lips worked as she tried to decipher whatever it was the imp had said. "I'm sorry. I don't understand that. Can you repeat?"

Brimbibor had lifted his trident up, aiming the tips at the sugar fairy with a gleaming, predatory grin. He blinked. "Ghung?"

"Um. I don't really understand what you're saying," Sugressa pressed on. "I'm sure you're not eating mashed potatoes right now, but it kinda sounds like you are. Maybe finish it first and try again? I can wait."

Brimbibor's overhanging brow scrunched in on itself in a frown. He tilted his head to the side. "Ghung hesh bormishkavork bumboshlogen borkiba shorgern flergenox."

While Sugressa continued to push Brimbibor's mind to its intellectual limit, Fecanya took the opportunity to circle around to his side. She set her wings buzzing and flew straight for the imp's exposed ribcage.

"Ghung?"

Time, once again, grabbed popcorn and began to weave yet another masterpiece of misfortune.

Brimbibor noticed Fecanya just in time to be too late for the both of them. "Ghilgenshirk!" Despite his best effort to move out of the way, he only managed to lean away from the speeding missile that was Fecanya.

Having noticed the hulking imp leaning away from her, Fecanya tried to alter her trajectory, which meant pulling up.

Imp and fairy shared the simultaneous moment of misfortune in a brilliant dance of speeding slow motion.

Trident still over his head, Brimbibor yelled in panicked dismay as he leaned away to escape the collision he knew he couldn't.

Fecanya gritted her teeth into a snarl and pulled up to keep in line with Brimbibor's ribcage. Unfortunately, the way in which he'd leaned away set Fecanya in a direct route for his furry armpit.

"Guhuunghk!"

"Oomph!"

The moment of face-to-armpit collision lasted an instant and a lifetime, allowing Fecanya not only to fully sample the robust pong of Brimbibor's humid armpit, but that, mingled with the acrid mist generated from his responding exhalation.

"Mmph by Lilith's bloody underworld," Fecanya's muffled voice swore. She balled her fist and rammed it into Brimbibor's nether region.

Like the whistle of a deflating balloon, Brimbibor squealed and folded himself around Fecanya's fist.

"Ugh, get *off*!" She braced her feet against Brimbibor's side and shoved until she got her arm free.

Brimbibor responded by slowly sinking to the ground like a stone in water, where he lay on the ground, drowning in crotch pain.

"Stinking lummox." She wiped the tears from her eyes and tried to will the smell of fur smothered in onions and rotten garlic out of her nose.

"There's more coming," Sugressa said. "We need to leave now."

Fecanya looked over her shoulder to see a swarm of bat-winged imps flopping in their direction, spears in hand. She coughed and lurched sideways.

Sugressa grabbed her arm and held her upright, then swished her wand in front of Fecanya's face. The smell of fresh roses and sweet buns choked out Brimbibor's putrid scent, and Fecanya felt her strength returning.

"Let's go!" Vegetina said. I don't mind a fight, but not with these odds.

They fled, zipping between trees and branches and poles. Bits of black magic rained down around them as the imps gave chase. Several voices squealed in recognition behind them.

"Seems they dislike you on a personal level," Vegetina remarked.

"Can't imagine why," Fecanya replied.

They picked up the nymph's trail just outside of town and sped back into the woods, hooting, cursing imps in their wake.

TWENTY-ONE

The imps caught up to them deep in the woods. Fecanya dodged a stabbing spear and grabbed the offending imp's wrist. She twisted inward, causing the imp to bend forward, then dealt it an uppercut in the throat.

Vegetina delivered a flying haymaker to the side of an imp's head that sent it speeding into its nearby companion. Both went down in a heap.

Sugressa being the passive fairy that she was, shuddered at the thought of violence. Instead, she gently guided an attacking imp around her person and into the trunk of the tree behind her. She pretended the resulting "crunch" was a bag of potato chips it had in an invisible pocket somewhere instead of its nose.

Imps and fairies darted between the trees, black magic and fairy magic zipping through the air. Fecanya spotted an imp who'd flown high overhead and was now diving straight for her. With a gesture and a waggle of her fingers, she drew the pollen from several dozen tree leaves and sent it funneling toward the imp. With her other hand, she made a similar gesture toward the ground below.

While the pollen funneled with surgical precision into the imp's nostrils, a cluster of deer pellets lifted from under a bed of leaves. What came next was the beginnings of a sneeze that ended in a choking scream of revulsion.

Having taken her immediate enemy out of the fight, an idea flashed in Fecanya's mind. "Hold on!" she yelled to the scattered fairies. She could only hope everyone heard. "Take cover when you get the signal."

"What signal?" Sugressa asked.

"You'll know when you hear it."

Vegetina gritted her teeth and slugged an imp in the jaw. As her now unconscious foe's body spun counterclockwise, she drew her wand and blasted an incoming imp in the face with a fist-shaped stalk of broccoli. "Hurry up!"

Fecanya was already on the move. She searched the sky with her senses.

As nature would have it, ordure engineers had a special affinity with organisms who specialized in the weaponization of their personal leavings. This included all manner of nonhuman—in most cases—primates, seagulls, and especially, lorikeets.

Fecanya couldn't believe her luck. Not only had she found a flock of seagulls, which in itself wasn't wholly unusual, but that she'd also found a flock of lorikeets. If there was one thing humans did exceptionally well, it was welcome whole species into non-native regions, especially those who were good at reproducing.

She rubbed her hands together and sent out her thoughts to the leaders of both avian flocks. She headed back toward the fight, not waiting for a response. The little parrots and gulls would follow. They couldn't help it. The birds took pleasure in relieving themselves in most creative ways.

In the short time it took her to contact the birds, several imps had caught up to her. Fecanya waved her hands in a quick pattern and, with a flick of her wrist, sent a powerful gust of wind into them.

While imps share the same type of wings as bats, they do not, however, share their aerial agility. The gust was enough to send the maladroit creatures careening into one another with expletive-ridden tangle of limbs and wings.

The harsh cry of a dozen seagulls drew Fecanya's attention higher in the sky. The white and gray birds angled in her direction. Riding their wake glided a rainbow-colored flock of grinning lorikeets.

The little parrots let out a screech of glee; all but the lead parrot who simply shouted "you SHTINK."

Fecanya flew in line with the birds and as they passed, she grabbed hold of the lead seagull and rode it down toward the woods and her fleeing companions.

At her higher vantage point, Fecanya nodded in appreciation of Sugressa's and Vegetina's agility. They zipped between branches, around tree trunks, and through bushes. They dodged stabbing and thrown spears while managing the occasional counterattack.

An imp caught up to Sugressa and drew back his spear, thus leaving his midsection open.

"Oh!" Sugressa ducked and covered her head with her hands, conveniently placing her rather sharp elbow in line with its midsection. She clamped her eyes shut and dove toward the imp, placing herself safely inside the reach of its spear, and her elbow safely in line with its solar plexus.

"Ghrgph!"

Sugressa opened her eyes and looked up, directly into the eyes of the imp that looked as though it were losing the battle to retain its lunch.

A shadow rolled over the woods followed by the screech of a sizable flock of seagulls. Riding astride the lead gull was Fecanya, her short, auburn hair whipping in the wind above her wild-eyed smile.

"Oh dear." Sugressa looked from the seagull to the sagging imp and back. "Oh dear. I'll ... I'll just go over here." She flew to the side as fast as her wings could take her. The guilt of leaving her attacker in the line of fire stood no chance against her desire to not be *in* said line of fire. "Vegetina! Take cover!"

Vegetina released the imp she had in a headlock. "Hm?" She looked up and her eyes widened in terror. She planted her feet against the gasping imp's back and pushed off. Her wings beat furiously as she raced for the nearest oak. She whipped around the trunk and planted her back against it.

The imps had started to give chase when several stopped and looked to the sky.

"Aye. Durginfresh. Wassat?" Flapping beside his companion, an imp shifted his club to his other hand and pointed a bony finger at the avian swirl getting closer.

Durginfresh wouldn't be considered intelligent by most sentient terms, but he was smarter than the average imp. "What're you mumblin' about, Horglyn?" He looked to the sky and his beady black eyes glazed over. "No! Get away, you fools! Get awa—" he tried to fly away only to crash into Horglyn. "Get away, get away!"

Seagulls screeched. Imps screamed. Fecanya's wild laughter drowned them all out.

Thuds and splats mingled with horrified cries of mercy and retreat as avian bombers pulled up from their dive and released their payloads. In the ensuing chaos, the lorikeet squadron glided into the trees and took up positions in an arc in front of the disoriented creatures.

"You SHTINK!"

The lorikeets hopped in an about face, their backs to the drenched and flailing imps.

Dragging Sugressa by the wrist, Fecanya found Vegetina pressed against the trunk of an oak. She looked up at Fecanya, eyes wide and chest heaving. "Is it over?"

Fecanya grabbed her wrist and pulled them both into flight. "Trust me. You don't want to be anywhere near ground zero."

"But," Vegetina argued, "what if those parrots need help—"

"Trust me; you'd feel sorry for the imps if you knew—"

"You shtiiiiiiiink!" the lead lorikeet shouted.

"Why does that parrot only say that?" Vegetina asked. She looked down at all of the forest animals sprinting away from the area. Squirrels, deer, and rabbits breezed past them in near panic.

Fecanya shrugged and almost got clipped in the shoulder by a fleeing pigeon. "Probably the only thing its humans taught—"

The sound of rapid-fire flatulence and heavy impacts drowned out the rest of what she said.

All three fairies scrunched their faces in an attempt to drown out the horrific sounds of the battle's conclusion behind them. It went on far longer than necessary, and Fecanya wondered if the parrots were actually enjoying it.

"My goodness," Sugressa said when the explosions ceased. "Do you think the imps are gone?"

"I can't imagine anything surviving what we just heard," Vegetina replied. "Best we go make sure, though. Don't want to leave our allies to fight without us."

Fecanya waved her hands. "No. No. I think we should leave. All should be fine."

"You wanna just leave without making sure they're not in trouble. Birds can't exactly fight off a bunch of imps."

"I guarantee you those imps want to be anywhere but where they were just moments ago."

"She's right, Fecanya," Sugressa said. "We should make sure they don't need our help."

Fecanya looked into Sugressa's bright, naive eyes, and sighed. "Suit yourself."

They passed many animals and birds on their way back, none of which were interested in returning.

"I could swear those ravens were snickering at us," Sugressa said.

"They think we're crazy," Fecanya said.

"Why would they think that."

The answer came in the form of Vegetina's nauseated gulp.

"Oh ... my," Sugressa breathed.

"How can a dozen small birds wreak this kind of destruction?" Vegetina said. "It looks like an army of humans with paint guns were here."

"You all right?" Fecanya asked. "You look a little green in the face."

Vegetina turned away and swallowed. "M'yeah I'll be fine."

Fecanya heard a sigh from her other side and turned just in time to catch Sugressa as she fainted.

TWENTY-TWO

"You are in deep trouble, young lady." Bloomara glowered at the forest nymph as she sauntered by her barred cell. "You have no idea what you've done."

Though she made a show of confidence, Bloomara hardly felt it. She looked about their dank surroundings with dismay. The nymph had bound them in vines that had carried them inside the massive oak. It seemed large enough for a band of dwarves to huddle in, though she was sure the odor would take up considerable space on its own.

"Actually," Siraka said. "I know exactly what I'm doing."

"Which is?"

Siraka put her hand on her hip. "Is this the part where I explain my master plan in detail for you to then think real hard on, so you can find a way to thwart me, Bloom Fairy?"

Bloomara nodded. "Well, that would make this whole thing run a lot more smoothly, yes."

Siraka blinked, then looked to Garbita, who offered a smile showing all her teeth. She shrugged. "Because it's fun."

"What?" Bloomara started to grab at the wood bars of her cell, then snatched her hands back. She looked at her now healed palms, then at the bits of iron sprinkled all about the bars. It had been a painful lesson. "Fun? Have you any idea the kind of chaos and destruction you've wrought?

Taking away their technology boxes is bad enough, but taking their caffeine? They'll destroy the world!"

"T ... technology boxes?" Siraka's green lips crinkled. "You know they're called computer's, right?"

Bloomara waved an irritable hand. "Whatever. It doesn't matter. You're going to have them destroy everything. And for what reason?"

Siraka made a show of thinking it over. "Have you never had fun with a human before."

Garbita gasped. "I assure you we've *never*—"

"Not *that* kind of fun. Don't get your bun wobbling again."

"My hair bun does *not wobble*! You truly need an edu*cation* in *manners*, young lady."

Siraka wobbled her head through Garbita's speech.

Garbita gnashed her teeth. "Pray I don't get out of this *cell*, you vine-wearing *harlot*."

Now Siraka burst into laughter. "See?" She looked to Bloomara while pointing at Garbita. "Humans are even easier than she is. It's a riot." She shrugged a shoulder. "And if I'm going to raise an army to help slap Mab around, I may as well have fun while I'm at it."

Bloomara and Garbita gasped.

"Easy, there," Siraka said. "Your eyes are going to pop out of their sockets if they widen any more."

"Now you see how insane she is." Caffeinisa sat with her back against the far wall of her cell, filthy, her black and gray jumpsuit torn in several places. She used a rather interesting choice of finger to swipe her raven bangs out of her face while glaring at Siraka. "This tart has it out for Queen Mab. *Queen. Mab.*"

"But ... but why?" Bloomara closed her eyes and shook her head as if to drive the fear away. "How?"

"Why?" Siraka laughed. "Because it's aaaaaall part of my plan to destroy the world!" She lifted her hand, palm to the sky, and curled her fingers. "With my army of evil nymphs and garden gnomes, I will set fire to this world and hurl the flames of ruin right into Queen Mab's uppity sidhe kingdom! I will wipe them ... from *existaunce*!"

Bloomara stared in silent horror. "You're insane. You are completely insane! Queen Mab is far too powerful ..." she stopped short when she heard Caffeinisa's sigh. "What?"

The caffeine fairy sighed again, and Bloomara looked back to Siraka. The nymph's lips were compressed into crinkled line, and the muscles in her stomach clenched as she held back a shudder of laughter.

Bloomara bared her teeth in a snarl. "When I get out of here—"

"You'll commit unspeakable pain upon my person. Ya, I know. Look, Mab is known by humans as the 'midwife of men's dreams'."

"*What* do you care about *that*?" Garbita asked. "That business is between *her* and any human *foolish* enough to make *deals* with her." Bloomara moved back from the cell bars when Siraka's nostrils flared.

"I wouldn't be angry at all if that was the extent of it." For a brief moment Siraka's green eyes blazed with anger. She seemed to catch herself and cleared her throat. "But when Mab's sense of humor involves me, I have a problem with it."

"What did she *do*?" Garbita asked. "*Surely* it must have been something *truly heinous* to invoke such ire that you would enlist such smelly *creatures* to *aid* you in a *war*."

"You really have a flair for the dramatic, Garbage Fairy."

Garbita ground her teeth. "You—"

"Ahem, you said something about involving you?" Bloomara interrupted before Garbita could get going. "Did Queen Mab do something to you?"

"Oh, she did something all right." Siraka made a gentle upward wave of her hand. Vines slithered out of the shadows of the little makeshift tree dungeon. They coalesced into a throne which she hopped into and crossed her legs.

"You ever see what human's dream about?"

"Dream about?" Bloomara shook her head. "I can't say that I do."

"You're lucky. Unfortunately for me, a night out drinking with the illustrious Mab landed me in a dingy apartment where the rodents begged me for a way out, and shacked up with a drunken sea captain with a musty beard, dirty fingernails, and extreme halitosis."

Bloomara wrinkled her nose. "How in Lilith's underworld did you land yourself in that situation?"

"I already told you. Mab has a sense of humor only she appreciates." Siraka glowered at a distant memory. "I'd met with her because she'd hired me to decorate some of the walls in her queendom with ivy. I'd been there for several days and we'd gotten to know each other. Started to hang out, go drinking, blah blah blah." She ended with a disgusted snort.

Bloomara frowned in sympathy. "Dear me. Out drinking with Queen Mab. Any of the other royalty would have been a safer excursion."

"How nice it would have been to know that, sooner," Siraka said. "Anyway, a few too many drinks and a few too many jokes. I had to open my fat mouth about how I didn't like the smell of fish, and how sea captains smelled like fish walking on land." Siraka bared her teeth. "If only I'd known what that grin had meant when I saw it.

"Long story short, she actually found a drunken sea captain at the wharf who happened to smell like he'd been swallowed by a large fish. And, as my beautiful luck would have it, he'd had a secret wish that elves were real, and that he could have a tumble with an elven woman."

Bloomara blinked. "But you're not an—"

Siraka held up a hand. "We're talking about a man who grows his own personal mildew garden under his arms."

"Dear me," Bloomara whispered.

"So, a night of drinking, a misplaced comment, and I'm magically bound to bouncing on the knee of Sardine Sam while having to hear the disembodied laughter of my supposed friend."

"Have you thought of talking to the queen to tell her how that made you feel?"

Siraka gave her a blank look. "Mab enjoys toying with everyone and you know it. The more annoyed I became, the harder she'd laughed. I swore I'd make her pay for that."

"So," Bloomara said, carefully. "You've indirectly sown chaos in the human population to provide enough energy for minor devils to enter this world? But, Mab doesn't live in this world. Nothing you do there will affect ... oh dear."

Garbita frowned. "What?"

"Dear me. No." Bloomara shook her head. "Look. Whatever grievance you have against Queen Mab, there must be a better way to resolve it. If you bring those abysmal creatures from their world into this one, you won't get them all to faerie. Some are going to slip away. And the ones that you *do* get to faerie, what then? Tear down the whole queendom over a grudge?"

"Yup."

"And you think you can control all of those smelly creatures?" Bloomara looked pleadingly at the nymph. "Think about what you're doing, Miss Siraka. If you succeed, the queendom of Mab will be overrun with those vermin. If you fail, Queen Mab will not be forgiving."

Siraka shrugged. "No risk, no reward."

"And just what *is* your reward in all this foolishness?" Garbita asked.

Bloomara shot her a warning look.

"You know, Garbage Fairy." Siraka moved toward Garbita's cell, her vine throne deconstructing itself to follow behind. "You really need to learn how to talk to others."

"What ... what are you doing?" Garbita backed away from the bars as the vines slithered between them and into the cell. "You can't *do* this! Stop. Get those things away from ... mrgph!"

"Stop this instant!" Bloomara looked from Siraka to Garbita who was now wrapped in vines.

"Quite dramatic, you are." Siraka opened the door to the cell and walked up to Garbita, now held aloft by the vines, which had wrapped around her body and covered her mouth. She lifted her chin and stared into Siraka's eyes, her own blue orbs blazing with defiance.

"Please," Bloomara said. "We're not your enemies We just came to rescue our sistren. Please." She watched helplessly as the nymph sauntered up to Garbita. One of the vines slithered beside her and unwrapped itself, revealing a dagger.

"I promise this'll be quick and painless."

A tear rolled down Garbita's eye, but she held the nymph's gaze.

"That's right," Siraka said. "Be brave."

"Please." Bloomara sank to her knees. "Please don't do this."

"Think about what you're doing," Caffeinisa said. "This is madness, Siraka!"

"It's not too late," Siraka. The voice came from a cell in the far end of the chamber. Tootheria. "You haven't crossed the line yet. You can still turn—"

The knife rose and fell.

Bloomara clamped her eyes shut and screamed.

TWENTY-THREE

"Will. You. Please. Knock it off with the dramatics, Bloom Fairy? It's getting really annoying."

Bloomara cracked one eye open, then hopped up with a gasp.

The vines receded from a rather bewildered Garbita who was using her fingertips to first poke about her throat and midsection, then through the loaf of green hair at her scalp.

Siraka walked to a table in the shadows that Bloomara hadn't noticed before and dropped several green locks into a bowl. She glared over her shoulder at Bloomara. "All this howling and theatrics. You act like I was about to cut off all her hair and leave her bald, or something."

"Oh, I ..."

The forest nymph slowly turned to face her, hand ominously on her hip. "Huh." She poked her jaw out as she ran her tongue along the inside of her teeth. "Good to know how low an opinion you have of me." She took a threatening step forward. "Maybe I should shave *you* bald."

Bloomara's mouth bounced open and closed several times.

Caffeinisa whispered at her side, "Few things are more horrifying to a nymph than being bald. Play along with it before she decides to think of something worse."

"Oh, dear me, no! Please!" Bloomara placed her fingertips over her heart and took two high steps backward. "Please! You mustn't! I meant no offense." She made a show of tripping over her feet to fall gracefully to the floor.

Caffeinisa rolled her eyes. "Ya. Just like that."

"I don't know whether I'm being mocked, or you're really like," Siraka waggled her hand at Bloomara, "this." She stepped up to the bars, the vines following in her wake. "Look, just gimme a few locks of that mane of yours and we won't need the vine treatment. M'kay?"

"You *could* have offered *me* the same *option*," Garbita complained. She forcefully smoothed her crinkled green leaf dress.

"I *could* have, but I *didn't* because *my* way made you *quiet*." Siraka turned back to Bloomara and flipped the dagger in her hand. "You can do it or I can."

Bloomara rose to her feet and warily reached out to grab the dagger. Siraka grinned and bounced her eyebrows.

"What is this for?" Bloomara separated a few strands of hair and sliced them off. She swallowed, noting how easily, almost eagerly, the sharp blade cut through the locks. "Are you planning some sort of witchcraft?"

Siraka snorted. She held out her hand and Bloomara dropped her hair in it, then handed over the dagger, relieved to be rid of the dreadful thing.

"Let's just say it'll be your little contribution to the war effort."

Next came Caffeinisa, then Tootheria.

Siraka went to the farthest corner of the chamber to a cell separated from the others. A fairy with black and brown hair wearing the same-colored dress in a marble pattern glared at her over the gag stuffed in her mouth. "I s'pose you should just let me do it," Siraka said, indicating the fairy's bound wrists.

"That's ... is that Mewamina?" Garbita asked.

Bloomara nodded absently.

"But *why* does she have her *gagged* and tied *up* like that? She's no more *dangerous* behind these fool bars than *we* are."

"Not so, Garbage Fairy." Siraka waited while Mewamina leaned her head close to the bars. She reached through and sliced off a few brown and black locks. "As you already know, our friend here is responsible for teaching cats to mew. Which pretty much means she can communicate with the devious buggers."

Bloomara could practically feel Mewamina's icy cold glare at Siraka's back. She shivered. Mewamina's job might be cute in concept, but anyone who dealt with cats for a living was either incredibly stupid, or tough as dwarven baked bread. Mewamina was most definitely the latter.

After collecting hair from each of the incarcerated fairies, Siraka bent over her bowl and began mixing a multicolored liquid with it. Lastly, one of the vines slithered up to her side and she gingerly extracted a thin strand from it.

She slowly waved her hand over the bowl and a pungent mist drifted out of it. The room lit with multicolored flashes and the mist wafted from the bowl and spread across the chamber. It swirled around Mewamina, then made its way to Tootheria. After wrapping around the tooth fairy, it shot away and enveloped Caffeinisa.

The mist wrapped around Garbita. "Get this disgus—*cough*." She dropped to her knees and inhaled a deep wheeze, much like an asthmatic dragon. "*Cough cough!*"

After lingering around Garbita for what seemed like a sentiently sarcastic amount of time, the mist flowed away to lastly wrap around Bloomara. Its cold caress swept around her and between her wings—most inappropriately, to Bloomara's sensibilities—then hustled back into the bowl.

A great howl of wind filled the chamber and ended with a loud '*pop*'.

"Ah, finally." Siraka reached into the bowl and extracted a twisted stick as long as her forearm. Spiraling the length of the stick were strands the color of each of the captive fairies' hair.

"What in the name of Lilith's underworld is that?" Caffeinisa breathed.

Siraka winked at her. "I would have liked to have gotten a lock of your ordure engineer's hair, but this should do well enough."

Bloomara's eyes widened. "You've made a wand infused with our attributes. That is criminal! It's against the natural laws of—"

"I'm aware," Siraka said flatly. "But I also don't care. I'm taking this wand with as many of those smelly creatures I can round up, and I'm going to make Mab's life ... difficult."

"But ... Queen Mab will recognize our individual signatures in the magic you wield. You'll be implicating us in your scheme!"

Siraka looked at her, then looked at her new wand. She shrugged.

TWENTY-FOUR

"I don't like the look of those vultures that were staring at us," Sugressa whispered. She glanced over her shoulder as if to ensure the creepy birds weren't following them.

They'd been skulking along the shadowy tunnels in the great oak long enough for Fecanya to admit to herself that they may be lost. "Well it's not like they can climb in here after us. Just keep your eyes open, we're almost there."

"Does 'almost there' involve us passing that black and orange spider squatting on its web in a trunk knot several times?" Vegetina asked. "I think it was going to offer instructions but you blew by it too fast on our third lap."

"There's spiders everywhere in here, okay?" Fecanya ground her teeth and shouldered past the black and orange spider. It winked four of its eight eyes at her. She cleared her throat. "Ahemthiswayhurryup."

"Hold on," Vegetina whispered. "I think I heard something."

The trio froze midskulk and Vegetina lowered her ear to the floor. "I hear vines moving. Big ones."

"Oh no." Sugressa pressed her fists to her mouth. "They're not coming for us, are they?"

"No. They're responding to instruction. Most plants are stationary, but the ones like vines can actually do things if you know how to talk to them. The sound is coming from the right. So ... just stay against the wall to the right. Actually, just follow me."

Fecanya could feel the black and orange spider's smirk as she stepped aside to let Vegetina take the lead. The vegetable fairy led them through dimly lit tunnels and into darker ones. "Up there." She pointed to an opening overhead, then ascended with a flutter of her wings.

They joined her, and found themselves in a larger portion of the trunk, the darkness illuminated by the soft caress of fey light. Sugressa shrank away from the walls and practically climbed up Fecanya's back.

"Mmph, what are you doing, Sugressa?"

"They're everywhere." She pointed out the vines covering the walls and ceiling. They slithered about in every direction and seemed to take no notice to the crouched trio.

"Yes, they're everywhere," Fecanya hissed. "Now kindly get off me."

Vegetina was already on the move, heading in the same direction as some of the larger vines.

Fecanya trotted to catch up, Sugressa's terrified panting hot on the back of her neck. "Will you calm *down*," she hissed. "The humidity from your breath is making my hair frizz." She ran her fingers through her short, auburn hair as it rapidly transformed into an afro.

"Sorry, Fecanya."

Now feeling guilty, Fecanya turned and gave Sugressa a pat on the shoulder. "It's okay—"

"Oooh that's pretty! It's like a big round puff!" Sugressa's smile spread ear to ear. "Can I ..." she reached out a tentative hand toward Fecanya's head. "Can I touch it?"

Fecanya combed her fingers through her afro again. "Only if you like mangled fingers."

The golden glow of fey light grew brighter as they followed the vines, coming to a bend where they reached the far wall of the trunk. They finally reached an opening where the light was brightest. It spilled out into the dim area of the partially hollow trunk, coating the walls and most of the floor like a golden gloss.

"I hear voices," Vegetina said. "They're in there."

The trio tiptoed to the corner and peeked into the chamber. Rows of cells lined the walls, their bars made from the wood of the tree and encircled with enough bits of iron to keep the prisoners from trying to escape.

A rather annoyed-looking Mewamina sat cross-legged with back against the wall. In a cell a few feet away, Tootheria muttered something about having extra teeth for her collection if she ever got her hands on that nymph.

Further into the chamber against the far wall, a snarling Caffeinisa glared daggers at the floor in front of her. In the cell beside her, Bloomara stomped about while swinging her fists in the air. Beside her cell, Garbita sat against the wall, chin raised in elegant indignation.

Sugressa shivered. "Iron. Yuk. What'll we do?"

"Whatever it is, it'll have to be at a distance." Vegetina hugged herself. "I'd rather not break out in hives and itch for two weeks." She shook her head irritably. "Why'd it have to be iron?"

"You know very well why, my dear."

The fairies spun, Sugressa and Vegetina drawing their wands, Fecanya's hands already in motion.

Vines shot out of the darkness and encircled the trio. Several slim tendrils wrapped around Vegetina's ankle and yanked her off her feet. Sugressa swept her wand in the direction of the vines and hit them with a gust of fairy dust.

Stung, the vines shrank away, giving Vegetina enough time to hop to her feet. She straightened her back, lifted her chin, and took a tall, regal stance. Her wand held in a delicate grip between her fingers, she made subtle, flicking motions; a twitch here, a swirl there.

The vines shuddered in protest, but one by one, they bent to the vegetable fairy's will. The vines were her orchestra, and Vegetina, their conductor. She guided the vines away from the others and turned them against the nymph.

Siraka snarled and curled her fingers. The corded muscles in her arms flexed as she exerted her will on the dancing vines.

Back and forth the struggle went, Vegetina using her magic of affinity against the symbiotic magic that was the dryad's very nature.

Sweat trickled down the side of Vegetina's face. "I promise I won't mind if you hurry up," she said through gritted teeth.

"On it!" Fecanya closed her eyes and drew upon some of the moisture in the walls of the tree trunk. She coaxed the moisture out and swept it along the floor, drawing up as much dust and dirt as possible. Once she'd created a thick enough sludge, she guided it to the bars of Bloomara's cell.

There was just enough mud to coat three of the six bars of her cell door. Bloomara pushed the cell door open and scrambled out. "Good thinking, Fecanya." She rushed to join the fight.

Fecanya drained the moisture coating the bars and continued to drain the moisture out of the bars themselves until they were brittle enough to break free. She snapped one out, replaced just enough moisture to ensure durability, then used it as a lever to wedge between the bars of Garbita's cell and pry it open.

"What Bloomara said," Garbita growled as she rushed to the others.

Fecanya caught the tiny hint of a smile Garbita tried to hide as she ran off. She grinned and moved to Tootheria's cell.

She'd barely pried it open before the tooth fairy shot out and into the fray.

With a waggle of her fingers and a flick of her wrists, Fecanya freed Mewamina of her bonds. She'd just pried open Mewamina's cell when she felt the frantic urge to duck. A cluster of vines came together in the form of a flyswatter and slapped Mewamina back in just as she was exiting.

The Cat Communications Fairy hit the ground like an expletive-ridden rag doll. Fecanya zipped across the room and settled beside Vegetina, who had sunk to her knees. She'd still managed to keep the vines from dealing any lethal damage, but she was rapidly weakening.

Fecanya waved her hands and waggled her fingers at a cluster of vines slapping at Caffeinisa. Moisture flowed out of the vines, and they started to droop.

Siraka wailed and turned her venomous gaze on Fecanya. "You pest! You horrible, spindly-limbed flea!"

"Spindly-limbed?" Fecanya raised her eyebrows. "I'll bet these spindly limbs are strong enough to knock you asleep, tree trollop!"

"I'm going to ... *oomph!*"

Like a bolt of lightning, Caffeinisa flew fists-first, straight into Siraka's midsection. The dryad folded in half over her.

Being the unparalleled expert of "the perfect moment" that Time is, this indeed proved the perfect moment to slow and speed up at the same time, regardless of the impossibility of it all.

While Time had its fun, Siraka continued to double over at a speed that would have had Cruzindream the sloth tapping his foot with impatience. As her eyes widened and her mouth fell agape in a desperate but failed attempt to do anything but exhale more oxygen, Tootheria reached into the fanny pack strapped to her waist.

The tooth fairy pulled her fist free and hurled its contents at Siraka's face with deadly accuracy.

Being that Time was quite enjoying itself, Siraka was afforded a clear view of the tiny baby teeth speeding across the chamber. The horror crept upon her with the speed of a thousand tortoises that had gotten a bit into the "grass".

Siraka struggled to close her mouth, but such actions require time. And Time, however, had other ideas.

The teeth continued their trajectory and—against physics's strict rules of conduct—her eyes widened even more as the baby teeth gently deposited themselves into her mouth.

To her surprise—and dismay—Siraka's mouth returned to normal speed as soon as the little white projectiles entered. Her mouth shut with a click of her own teeth.

"Hak. HuuuHAK. HuuuuHAAAUUK."

"Oh my." Sugressa watched the gagging nymph with sympathy. That looks awful." She turned to Fecanya. "I think she's going to choke—"

"If we're lucky," Vegetina muttered as Fecanya helped her to her feet.

"Der slimy. Dyhuuuurgh." She scratched at her throat. "Der so slimy!"

"I know she's a dryad," Sugressa said, "but I never thought they could make their faces go that green."

"Get yourself a mouthful of those nasty little things and see what color your face turns," Caffeinisa replied.

"Urgh I think I just swallowed them all ..."

Tootheria lifted her chin. "They're just fine after you've given them a good cleaning."

"Ain't enough cleaning in the world for me to want to make a house out of human teeth," Caffeinisa said. "Can you imagine the smell?"

"There is no *smell*," Tootheria growled.

Siraka started to perform the heimlich maneuver on herself.

"Look, Toothie," Caffeinisa said. "Nobody's lookin' down on your job. I mean, it could be worse. It's not like you work with sh ..." she coughed and cleared her throat.

Siraka punched herself in the stomach.

"You do know that some of the coffee stuff you work with is dragged through the intestines of primates, right?" Fecanya replied.

"Oh don't get yourself in a sassy huff," Caffeinisa said. "We all have our jobs and they're all of value."

Fecanya rolled her eyes.

"I'm going to hurt you," Siraka growled. She glowered at them, and while the sight of her throat working to contain the revulsion lessened the impact, she nevertheless made a good show at willingness to back up the threat. She brandished her new wand.

"What in Lilith's underworld is *that* thing?" Fecanya asked. "It's pulsing with power. Lots of it."

"She *created* it out of a *mixture* of *all* of our *abilities*," Garbita said. "It is an abomi*nation*."

"Ugh. We're in trouble." Vegetina jerked and nearly slipped out of Fecanya's grip. "I've lost my hold on the vines."

Siraka flicked her wand at Bloomara. A speeding line of magical baby teeth thumped into her forehead, one after another. The missiles sent Bloomara feet-over-head into a backflip to crash unceremoniously to the floor.

Caffeinisa drew her wand but Siraka was faster. The teeth swirled away from the unconscious Bloomara and zipped in an arc toward the back of Caffeinisa's head, to similar result.

Vegetina's eyes grew distant as she no doubt tried to regain control of the vines.

Siraka waved her wand toward the vegetable fairy, and a green mist drifted under her nose.

"Oh ... *oh!*" Against proper judgement, Vegetina's nostrils widened. "Oh that's terrible! Terrible." She covered her nose, but the green mist simply drifted between her fingers.

The others had already begun to act, including the vines. Fecanya had managed to hit the dryad with a shot of magic, but Siraka merely stumbled. Several vines swirled into a cushion behind her and propped her up. She swished her wand in Fecanya's direction, and a swirl of fey magic plowed into her.

Twenty-Five

Fecanya hesitantly awoke from dreams of white sand beaches and margaritas. She creaked her eyes open and groaned. Her companions lay sprawled about the chamber as well, some picking themselves up off the floor while others were just coming to. "What happened?"

Caffeinisa pressed a hand against the side of her head, the other she used to wave at the room. "We fell asleep while knitting."

Fecanya rolled over onto her back and stared at the ceiling. "You all right, Sugressa?"

"I think so. Thank you for asking."

"Urgh." Mewamina climbed up to her hands and knees and looked in surprise at her not only present, but undamaged wand. "Considering she kicked the crap out of us, why'd she leave our wands here without at least breaking them?"

Garbita eyed her wand as if it were a venomous serpent. "Per*haps* she *sabotaged* them."

"I think I can answer that," Caffeinisa said. She rose and smoothed the legs of her jumpsuit, brushing dust off her top. "I drew out some of that moisture Fecanya'd collected from this chamber and combined it with some personal fairy dust. Gave her a nice big dose to wash down those baby teeth." Her face twisted into a devious grin.

The others cringed.

Fairies had their nasty little secrets as much as the next species, particularly when it came to fairy dust. There was the general fairy dust that nonfairies were aware of, but there was the personal stuff as well. Caffeinisa was, of course, the Pep Distributor, aka: Caffeine Fairy.

"Teeth swirling around in liquid caffeine laced with mud?" Mewamina hugged herself and shivered. "I'm surprised she didn't go for the big spit all over the floor."

"Well, she did make some sort of warbling sound and took off." Caffeinisa pointed in the direction Fecanya and the others had entered. "That way."

"Let's go over what we know so far," Bloomara stated.

"I would rather do it outside of this creepy place," Garbita said. She eyed the vines clinging to the walls and ceiling, pretending to be inanimate. "The more distance between us and those dreadful things, the better."

Vegetina led the way back, suspiciously slowing down as they passed the black and orange spider that pointedly looked at the space above Fecanya's head as she flew by.

"Perhaps just a bit farther away," Bloomara suggested when they stopped. She looked over her shoulder at the vultures still loitering on the branches overhead. "I don't like the look of them. For all we know, those thugs could be working for the dryad."

Several hooked beaks swiveled in their direction, and Bloomara shrank away.

"You really know how to make friends, Bloom," Fecanya said.

They found an empty heron's nest and settled in a circle, whereupon Bloomara stepped into the center. "Now then. We know that Siraka has gone quite insane. That much is clear. The best course of action would be to notify Fey World Maintenance Services to launch a simultaneous formal investigation and retrieval."

"Or," Caffeinisa said, "we could chase her down and stop her from infesting the area with imps before they trash the place on their way to Queen Mab's domain."

"Yes, of course," Bloomara went on. "But it is protocol that we first report to home base of the events—"

Mewamina put her fist to her mouth and coughed. Vegetina stared at nowhere in particular, while Tootheria watched with her mouth hanging open.

Fecanya felt a sudden rush of sympathy for Bloomara, who pushed on in spite of the rather ... tepid reactions to her suggestion. "I can't think of anyone more suited for that task than you, Bloom. You're the best at giving reports, so you can bring Harmass up to speed while we chase down Siraka. Harmass will know exactly the kind of help to send us, since she'll have the best info."

When Bloomara cast her a suspicious look she added, "or do whatever."

"This sounds like a good plan," Mewamina said. "Home base needs to know about this but we can't afford to give Siraka more time. She's probably got more of the things in this dimension, stinking up the place as we speak."

"Right then," Garbita said. "You give your *report*, Bloomara, and *we* chase down that forest *harlot*."

"This sounds a little personal, Garbita," Fecanya said.

Garbita sniffed. "She *stole* part of my *magic* and infused it in that ridiculous *wand* of hers. I plan to give her a good drubbing."

"It's settled," Fecanya said. "Bloom gives the report and we go drub the dryad."

Bloomara's mouth opened and closed while everyone agreed with the plan. She put her fists on her hips, but Sugressa gave her a hug. "Thanks, Bloomara! I know it's boring having to give a report, but you're the best at that sort of thing. It's why you're Head Fairy!"

"Mmph. I suppose you're right." Bloomara turned to the others. "We will—"

Half the fairies had already taken wing, only Fecanya, Sugressa and Garbita remaining.

"Um ... right then." Garbita jabbed a finger over her shoulder. "I think they've *caught* her *scent*. Best we get moving."

"You think she's upset?" Sugressa asked as they caught up to the others.

"Feel free to go with her," Fecanya suggested. She and Garbita glanced at her.

Sugressa made a show of thinking about it. "Um, I don't think I will. No, I don't think that's a good idea. I think I'm needed here. I'm sure Bloomara will be just fine giving her report."

And she and Lieutenant Commander Hardass can have pumpernickel croquets together while they discuss it, Fecanya thought.

"They've stopped," Garbita said, just as they reached the others.

"Looks pretty bad," Caffeinisa said.

Fecanya followed her gaze to see a town embroiled in chaos. Toilet-papered homes stretched into the distance, water gushed from broken fire hydrants which caffeine deprived humans attempted to make coffee from.

Glutenists clubbed Disorganizationists with French bread spears while the latter clubbed them with whatever came to hand.

"There!" Mewamina pointed at a group of imps squatting on a rooftop overlooking the fiasco.

"Little giggling bastards," Tootheria grumbled. "They think all this is funny."

"Well, it kinda is," Fecanya and Vegetina replied in unison.

"Until they start tearing up stuff that's not theirs," the tooth fairy countered.

"Because surely they don't do that now," Mewamina shot back.

"Let 'em go long enough without their caffeine and distractions," Caffeinisa said. "You'll be asking to sweep the floors in Lilith's underworld to get away from the place."

"There she is." Fecanya pointed to a redwood tree where Siraka lured a human out of the conflict and behind a tree. As she kissed him, a vine of poison ivy wrapped around him from head to toe for only a moment, then slithered away. Siraka let her fingers drag away from his chin and she left him there, flopping on the ground like a beached catfish, scratching every inch of his body.

TWENTY-SIX

The brisk afternoon air washed over Fecanya's face as she and the other fairies flew into battle. Magic tingled at her fingertips. On her left, sugar dust wafted from Sugressa's beating wings, lines of worry creasing her normally cheerful features. "You gonna be all right?"

Sugressa nodded, then shook her head. "I don't like this, Fecanya."

"We've dealt with these imps before," Fecanya said. "Nothing we don't know how to handle."

"Yeah but ..." she shook her head again. "If Siraka was able to bring them through so easily, what else—"

Space itself groaned in protest as a tiny black dot appeared above a Tabatha's Jewelry Store. The dot expanded, doubling itself over and over to the continued complaints of space and dimensional law.

"Uh ... ooooooooh." Sugressa pointed a trembling finger at the black space that was more house-sized hole than dot.

Tootheria bit her top lip. "Fan-friggin-tastic. She had to bring in a big smelly one."

Humans have countless myths about portals opening up from the bad places where a particularly frightening demon's foot—fully equipped with various built-in tools for slicing and impalement on each digit—drifts out of it. A rather large and thick leg attached to said foot would follow, depositing said foot to the ground with a mighty quake.

Big, gnarled hands equipped with similarly lethal cutlery would come next, gripping the sides of the portal despite the fact that one did not actually grip the sides of something with no physical presence. But then, there are no physics courses to attend in the demon realm so you just kinda went with what seemed right.

A loincloth made of the fur of a lesser demon would appear next—demons always climbed out of portals legs and hips first—followed by a head with sharp, angular features, a goatee precise enough you could slice a mean hunk of cheese with, pointed eyebrows, a finely pointed mustachio, and a nose pointing down in disdain at all before it.

Eyes the color of molten lava would look for the nearest unfortunate soul close enough to impale with the curving horns protruding from its forehead.

This particular demon, however, hadn't read any of the myths, and so it had grown a rather bushy eyebrow in place of forehead horns. Its green, moss-like hairline had been in full retreat for some time, and what was left, hung for dear life in a greazy—it had passed "greasy" status eons ago—mullet that hung limply around the cinnamon bun-like patch of skin on the back of its neck.

The yellowing nails that armed its fingers weren't sharp in the traditional manner, but rather, cracked and left with jagged edges that could surely draw a good bit of blood.

Last to come into view were its feet, due to it entering the earth realm headfirst. It crashed through the roof of the Tabatha's Jewelry Store all the way to its knees—which were in need of a good bit of the lotion—and feet that provided a healthy home for various fungi, much like barnacles on the chin of a whale.

Fecanya squinted across the distance at the newly arrived demon. "Uh oh."

"What is it?" Garbita asked.

"It's an Okradude." She pointed at what first looked like long locks of hair matted together but were in fact, strands of slimy, overcooked okra pods.

"Hommmm, hommmm, hommmm. Amma amma ammaaaaaa. Hommmm, hommmm, hommmm. Amma amma ammaaaaaaaa ..."

Fecanya looked in the direction of the sound to see the entire force of Glutenists kneeling in the street, arms extended over their heads, and repeatedly raising and lowering their faces to the—rather unclean—asphalt. "This is unbelievable."

"What're they doing?" Sugressa yelled. She ducked a stabbing spear aimed at her head and blasted the attacking imp in the face with a puff of baking flour. It fell away, wheezing and coughing up a white cloud.

"Those ..." Fecanya shook her head. "Those freaking primates are worshiping the Okradude! They're worshiping it!"

Garbita placed a hand to her mouth. "Oh dear. This is terrible."

"This is awesome," Caffeinisa yelled. "Are you joking? Look at it!" She pointed at the still bowing Glutenists, her mirth barely contained. "Look at them! This is great!"

"You have a rather *questionable* concept of *great*," Garbita replied.

Having been closer to the newly arrived demon, the Disorganizationists had begun to flee. To a person, however, their initial terror had been briefly overshadowed by disbelief at the kneeling and bowing Glutenists. They jogged to a stop and stared open-mouthed at the praying bread people, looked back at Okradude—or rather, its flailing potato-like feet—then looked at each other.

The sound of groaning and crumbling mortar rumbled out of the ruined jewelry store.

The Disorganizationists spared one last glance down at the now prostrate Glutenists, shared a disbelieving grin between themselves, and skipped sideways into a run.

If the worshipping Glutenists knew their former enemies had been and gone, they gave no indication. When Okradude finally began to right itself and stepped out of the rubble, its new worshippers' chanting grew more fervent.

The giant demon looked down at them, and the Glutenists sat up on their knees and raised their hands toward Okradude, their mouths agape in awe.

"We have fought for you, oh God of Gluten!" the leader of the cult declared. "We have battled your enemies and smote your nonbelievers! And with you to lead us, *now*, we shall preach your message and extend your reach to every corner of the world. This world will know the power and wonder of ..." he glanced around. "Bread!"

The bread cult touched their foreheads to the ground again, then straightened and raised their hands to the sky once more.

"Umphorghund." Okradude took a step toward its kneeling subjects and a smile dribbled across its face.

Humans worshipped a myriad of things, from Gods, to demons, jewelry, and even certain types of cheese. There was even a demon of taxes that was gaining in popularity among certain sections of the human populous, and word had it that a new Coffee God was picking up steam.

No one worshiped Okra, which meant among the many successful demons, Okradude was that guy who was allowed to hang around as long as he didn't talk to anyone or laugh too loudly at the jokes.

Okradude ran its dull-eyed gaze over its worshippers with growing pride. It wasn't exactly sure what gluten—or bread—was, but it wasn't asking questions.

When the humans raised their hands in praise again, Okradude gingerly reached down and plucked a woman from the crowd. It smiled at her screams of rejoice. The way the woman flailed her arms and legs with delight to the point that her bread helmet fell from her head filled Okradude with pride.

Air and ground rumbled under the weight of Okradude's powerful voice. "Bumhorgh." It plucked out a pod of okra from the back of its head and gave the woman in its fingers a little squeeze.

When her mouth fell agape, Okradude gently shoved the pod of into it.

"We have to do something!" Sugressa said. "It's going—"

"I've never seen a human's face turn yellow," Fecanya said.

Caffeinisa shivered. "If you had an overcooked okra spear shoved in your mouth you'd turn all kinds of colors."

Sugressa swallowed and drifted backwards, her fists to her mouth. "Why ... why doesn't she just spit it out?"

"The slime," Vegetina answered. "It's a sort of binding agent with elasticity. Once it's in your mouth, it clings. If you try to open your mouth, the slime will pull it shut. This happens over and over again until you've eventually chewed and swallowed the stuff."

"*Torture* by forced masti*cation*?" Garbita's eyes went wide with horror. "We must stop this ... that ..."—she flapped her hand—"that *thing*."

One by one the fairies drew their wands—Fecanya settled for cracking her knuckles—and zipped across the final distance and into the fray.

Formerly assaulting each other with baked weapons and rocks, the two human factions united in their mutual terror.

Okradude's first victim knelt on hands and knees, heaving on a nearby lawn. Her back arched in both directions as though performing yoga in fast forward.

The Glutenists looked at each other, then at the last of the Disorganizationists who were already in full flight, and took off after them.

Caffeinisa decked an imp square in the jaw and sent it careening into a nearby lightpost. She ducked a wild left hook by an imp behind her, locked its arm in hers, and gave it a twist. The imp howled and she hooked her index finger into the side of its mouth. She yanked it in front of her and held on just as Sugressa let fly a blast of sneeze sparkles.

With circular flourish of her wand, Garbita swept scattered magazines, soda cans, and cardboard boxes into a spinning cone. She lifted the street detritus into the air and sent it down an alley.

The litter cone crashed into the midst of a clump of imps egging on a pocket of fighting Glutenists and Disorganizationists who somehow hadn't noticed the appearance of a forty-foot-tall demon force-feeding overcooked okra to anyone too slow to get away.

The garbage scattered the imps and sent the fighting primates in a howling retreat.

An imp jabbed its spear at Fecanya and she spun aside. She grabbed the shaft, yanked the imp in close, and slugged it with a right hook. She grabbed it before it could fall away and swung it in a circle. She let go, and the imp crashed into several of its fellows.

While the jumbled creatures fought each other, Fecanya extended her awareness and found several deer deposits just outside the little town.

"Ugh."

"Argh!"

Thunk. Thunk. Thunkthunkthunkthunkthunkthunkthunk.

Furry limbs thrashed and bat wings flopped under the rapid-fire assault of petrified deer pellets.

"YeeeeeeeeAAAAAAAAaaaaaaah!"

Fecanya heard the scream and threw herself aside. A speeding imp zipped past her and crashed into its comrades, scattering them like bowling pins. Caffeinisa winked at her, then smacked an imp across the head with her wand. After the imp finished its resulting somersault, she blasted it in the face with a magical caffeine puff.

The imp inhaled the dust and its chin quivered. "Tzzzzzzzzz-ZZZZZZZYEHA hehHYA!" The imp flew in a circle like an explosive donut, then shot straight across the street and into a nearby wall.

"Aumbuhurgh!" Okradude held a hand over its right eye and swatted at Tootheria with its other hand, which still held the screaming Glutenist. The tooth fairy easily flew out of reach and shot it in the forehead with round after round of glowing, transparent teeth.

The sting of the little tooth bullets forced the demon to stumble backwards. It dropped the woman and threw its arms up to ward against the assault.

Vegetina conjured several huge bananas just behind its foot.

Once again, being the indiscriminate opportunist, Time slowed the moment to ensure all present were able to adequately appreciate what happened next.

"Mmmorghahungt!"

The instant Okradude's foot touched the magical bananas its speed multiplied, but Time was an infallible paradox.

While Okradude sped in slow motion into a painful splits, fleeing Glutenists stumbled over their own bread bowl helmets and tumbled into the street. Disorganizationists spilled into the avenue with them, all thoughts of their random conflict forgotten.

"Look what we've got, here!"

Fecanya whirled to see the imp they'd fought before, his sidekick Brimbibor flapping next to him. The smaller imp grinned gleaming sharp teeth at her.

"Ugh. Can't you idiots keep steady?" Fecanya asked. "All that bouncing up and down is making me dizzy."

"They can't," Vegetina said, hovering beside her. "Look at those dingy wings. They can barely keep airborne."

"You think you're funny?" the smaller imp replied, his grin widening. "I betcha ole Vincent and Brimbibor'll have the last laugh!"

Vegetina's mouth crinkled. "Vincent?"

"You're one to talk!" Vincent shot back. "You're named after your job. You all are. It's like the lot of you ain't got no imagination!"

"He's kinda right," Mewamina said. When Vegetina glared at her, she shrugged. "Our names are kinda on the nose."

Vincent's already widened grin widened further.

"Despite looking dumber the bigger his smile gets," Fecanya said,—Vincent's smile morphed into a scowl—"I have a bad feeling."

She'd barely finished talking when more portals opened and imps spilled through, swarming the town. What few human electronics still worked finally gave up. Streetlights flickered nauseatingly and all devices connected to the internet collectively screamed in the language of dialup.

"Oh, this is really bad," Vegetina said.

"Yup," Mewamina agreed. "And they've sabotaged warm showers, too."

Fecanya frowned at her. "How do you know that?"

"Humans emit a specific kind of wail when a warm shower turns ice cold. This is going to get a lot worse."

Another giant portal opened.

Twenty-Seven

T he fairies let out a collective sigh.

"What now?" Vegetina said.

"Maybe get over here and help me out," Tootheria yelled. She blasted Okradude in its other eye when the demon tried to get up. "Instead of hanging out and having high tea with those imbeciles trying to sneak up on you!"

The trio whirled just in time to see Vincent and Brimbibor flapping in their direction, Brimbibor's trident drawn back, Vincent's poison-tipped fingers curled.

"Gotcha!" Vincent shouted as he slashed his claws at Mewamina's face.

"Aren't you cute." Mewamina fluttered out of the way and as Vincent performed the equivalent of an aerial stumble past her, she slapped him in the back of the head.

Mewamina cupped her hands to her mouth and let out a loud meow as Vincent spiraled toward the ground.

A pack of alley cats appeared from the shadows and converged on the fallen imp. Vincent rose to his knees and gave his head a shake. He looked up and glared daggers at Mewamina, who smiled with an exaggerated wave.

Vincent's responding snarl crumbled at the sight of the cats surrounding him. He ran his tongue across his wolf-like muzzle and eyed the approaching felines.

The cats stalked in, their sadistic vertically slitted eyes trained on the tiny devil spawn.

Vincent took a frantic look around, then gathered himself and leapt into the air.

Or tried to.

A gray paw belonging to a rather large Maine Coon promptly snatched the imp out of the air and sent him spinning across the ground.

While cats settled into a circle and began their tennis match with Vincent, Vegetina threw herself into the side of Brimbibor's head just as the muscly imp had reached Fecanya. The two tumbled sideways and Fecanya flew to Vegetina's aid.

Together they rained blows down on the big imp's head, desperate to keep him from putting that trident to use. Their fists had little effect on the hulking Brimbibor, who shrugged off their blows and shoved them away. He pounded his chest, punched himself in the side of the head several times, and offered a toothy grin.

"Not much between his ears to damage," Vegetina muttered. She raised her fists. "Gonna be a tough one."

Fecanya snapped her fingers. "Almost forgot!" She focused her magic on some of the rubble from the petrified deer pellets scattered on the ground.

The Cervidae shrapnel raised into the air, combined into baseball-sized super pellet, and set a quick trajectory for Brimbibor's neither region.

Time was especially good at being forgotten until the instant came to release a particularly long running moment. At *this* moment, Time released its paradoxical hold on Okradude and sped up two points in space; the descent of Okradude's groin to the ground, and the meeting of the giant deer pellet and Brimbibor's crotch.

As the okra demon collided with the ground and began its soprano a cappella, the super pellet whizzed past the fairies, rustling Vegetina's hair, and collided with its target.

The resounding impact and Brimbibor's pitiful howl briefly paused the battle as fairy and imp alike gritted their teeth in collective sympathy.

Fecanya noticed Mewamina turn her horrified stare from the rapidly descending Brimbibor to her. She shrugged. "What else could I do? I stopped him, didn't I?"

On the other side of the small town opposite Okradude, a new arrival thrust its hips forward and lurched the rest of its body out of a portal. "Shermackerghen lerk," it said in a voice that made Fecanya think of a choking turkey.

The green, scaly demon looked around at the ensuing chaos and scratched its head. Dandruff in the form of bite-sized butter beans dislodged from its head and rained down on the fleeing populace.

When the screaming humans saw the arrival of the new giant, they tried to pivot away. Those behind them who hadn't noticed—due to running full on with head down and a perfect view of the ground—pushed them forward.

The first line of humans smashed butter bean dandruff underfoot as they struggled to turn away. The crowd behind them slipped on the trampled beans and fell unconscious. Those bringing up the middle and rear looked openmouthed to the sky.

Descending butter beans bounced off their faces, some finding their way into gaping mouths. They fell to hands and knees, heaving as their bodies instinctively tried to purge themselves of the scaly-skinned horrors.

Another portal opened. Dozens of grinning imps streamed out of the dark hole in the air and began hurling mushy chunks everywhere.

Sugressa pinched her nose. "What in Miss Lilith's Underworld is that smell?"

"This is bad," Fecanya said. "More imps and a Butterbean Flinger.

Vegetina looked around the head of the imp she was choking and nodded. "Very bad."

"What do you know?" Garbita asked. She delivered a whirling round-house punch into the ribcage of an imp, then swirled her wand in front of its face. Street garbage lifted from the ground and crashed into the imp and sent it flying away in a ball of cursing detritus. "What's happening over there?"

"They're heralds," Fecanya said. "Those little smelly devils are heralds!"

"For what?"

A demon about half the height of Okradude and Butterbean Flinger climbed out of a portal—hindquarters first—and whirled with a mighty yelp. Little green and yellow spikes covered its thickly muscled body, which heaved with malicious delight at the choking humans below.

Orange eyes widened with glee at the top of its noseless face, and it reached up and adjusted the spiky, yellow fruit helmet on its oval-shaped head.

"Oh my goodness!" Sugressa exclaimed. "It's a Durian Duke!" She whirled to face Fecanya. "I don't think we're powerful enough to stop it by ourselves. With those other two and the imps ..." she shook her head.

The Durian Duke let out a great belch. Human head-sized durian fruit chunks spewed from its maw and flew toward the slipping and sliding humans.

Fecanya worked her hands in a quick pattern. On either side of her, Garbita and Sugressa waved their wands as well. The trio created a gust of wind that redirected the projectiles and sent them crashing through the nearby imps to splatter against the wall of a building.

The resulting smell was instant.

"I think I'm going to be sick," Mewamina nasaled, her nose pinched between thumb and forefinger.

"It smells like someone let garbage and feet rot for a century and then dipped it in stagnant water," Caffeinisa said. She covered her face in the crook of her elbow.

"It's also really healthy," Vegetina replied. "There's a lot of health bene-fits to durian fruit."

"That's what makes this whole thing even more evil," Caffeinisa said from behind her cupped hand. She waved the other at the many gobs of durian fruit sliding down the walls around them. "To have to get through that smell to something healthy? Only a demon could accomplish that!"

"We're getting overrun," Sugressa said. "And I think the imps aren't bothering to be invisible anymore."

"Could be the sight of three towering demons trumps the presence of clumsy bat-winged imbeciles," Garbita said.

"Who you calling a windowsill?"

The fairies turned to see a disturbingly large gang of imps armed with spears, pitchforks, and perpetual grins flapping toward them.

"We can't fight all of them, those three giants, *and* the rest of those pests flying around the town," Caffeinisa said, as the fairies formed up into a line.

"The town's finished," Mewamina said.

"We're not in much better shape," Caffeinisa said.

Tootheria left the squirming Okradude and conjured a giant ball of enamel. She hurled the hard projectile at Butterbean Flinger. The magical enamel ricocheted into the side of Butterbean Flinger's head and made a straight course for Durian Duke's face.

Unfortunately, the durian demon was just belching another round of durian fruit as the enamel bolder was headed its way. The spiky fruit and the enamel collided in an explosion that sent chunks of the smelly fruit raining down on the town.

Already slipping and sliding on the butter beans in their flight, the terrified humans now struggled to keep their footing on the new layer of the durian.

The fairies hovered back-to-back, now.

"We can't win this fight," Fecanya said. "But we'll take as many of these annoying bastards down as we can, right, girls?"

"Guess this is it, then," Vegetina said. "You're a pretty good group to hang out with. Even you, Garbita."

"Well thank y ..." Garbita frowned.

Wave after wave of imps converged on the fairies and surrounded them while the three giants continued their rampage.

A horn sounded down the street, just beyond Terrence's Lumberjack Burgers 'N Fries.

Portals opened along the street, and out stepped dwarves, fairies, brownies, trolls, gnomes, and goblins.

Sugressa gasped. "It's our friends from FWMS! They've come to help!" Her pink hair and cotton candy-colored dress swished when she did a twirl of glee.

The imps' mischievous grins crinkled at the sight.

"She really is for real, isn't she," Vegetina whispered.

Fecanya nodded. "Yes, she is."

Somehow, Vincent had extricated himself from the mob of cats and had forced Brimbibor out of the fetal position and got him into the air. "This don't mean nothin'!" He pointed at the forces of FWMS. "C'mon, guys. Let's get 'em!"

Zachary Von Badass marched to the front of the goblin force and positioned himself between them and the dwarves. "You ... think ... *you* ... can defeat ... me? Aaaaaaaaah hahahahahaaaaaaaaa. Think ... again! It's time to unleash." He tore off his tank top to reveal muscles rippling like pebbles lining the bed of a raging brook. "Unleash ... THUH BHEAST!"

Beside Von Badass, Durgen Splurgenragher leaned away and snarled. "Watch where yer flingin' them spindly arms 'o yers, goblin, or I'll drop this axe and strangle yer neck."

If he'd heard the threat, Zachary Von Badass gave no indication. "You!" He pointed a long, skinny finger at the converging imps. "Aaaaall of you. You're gonna … feel … the PAIN. You're gonna feel … the pain … from all these … GAINS." He bent his front leg, half twisted his torso, and curled his arms downward.

"Anyone wanna tell me why we came in beside this idiot?" Davin Gravelchin asked.

Zachary opened his mouth—no doubt for another grand proclamation—just in time to receive a speeding gob of durian. His ears flapped over his face when his head snapped back.

As Zachary Von Badass's feet took to the air, the forces of Fey World Maintenance Services let out a war cry and charged.

The fey forces met in a jumble of floppy ears, stabbing spears, and swinging axes. Goblins punched imps out of the air. Imps smacked goblins across the backside, sending them into fits of pained circular hopping.

With no bare earth to work with, the gnomes had to improvise. They drew upon the soil in flowerbeds and gardens and hurled it into the mass of imps.

Fairies launched magical attacks, while taunting the dwarves who struggled against enemies far too small to hit with an axe.

Durgen Splurgenragher spat. "Plan B, boys 'n girls!" He strapped his axe across his back and drew a mallet from the buckle at his hip.

Axes were strapped to backs, mallets were drawn from hips, and impish grins rapidly disappeared.

From the nearby woods, a howl rent the not so silent night and a huge wolf appeared from the mist. Granted, the mist hadn't been there, moments ago, but it was mist's job to know when to add spice to an entrance.

"Uh oh," Daven Gravelchin said. He hefted his mallet and the imp on the business end of it slid free like a gob of butter. "It's a warewolf."

"There's no werewolves in these parts, dwarf," a nearby fairy drawled. "They live in the more remote forests."

"Yer right, sprite," Davin agreed. "That's why it ain't no werewolf. It's a durned warewolf. Just as bad, ye ask me."

The great brown wolf loped into the fray, grabbed a fleeing Glutenist and Disorganizationist, and bounded into a dark alley.

"We've got to save them!" the fairy said. She flicked her wand, and trapped a converging duo of imps into a sphere of ice.

"Nah," Davin said. He thrust his mallet forward and knocked out three imps midflight.

The toga-clad Glutenist and his Disorganizationist adversary cowered shoulder to shoulder, their backs pressed against the side of the building. Their only path of escape was blocked by the huge wolf that had brought them here.

It stood up on its hind legs at the mouth of the alley, its hungry, amber gaze holding them fast. Its muzzle trembled back into a snarl as it opened its maw to reveal two sets of sharp fangs. "Hold on one sec."

The two men glanced at each other, then looked back to the wolf, who was now pulling a cart behind it. It stopped in front of the two men and planted the kickstand on the cart.

"Sorry about snatchin' you up like that, but in the middle of all that chaos, you gotta think quick, you know?"

The two men's eyes widened, and they shrank away.

The wolf held out a paw. "Look, seriously, I'll make this worth your while. You." It indicated the Glutenist and reached into the cart. "Look, I know you guys do the toga thing ventilated ..." he snatched out a fresh pair of blue, green, and orange striped briefs. "But I *swear* these babies'll kick your mobility up a notch while lookin' stylish at the same time. Hmm? HMM?"

The Glutenist stared in paralyzed horror at the underwear. As his mouth started to formulate the words "no thank you", his eyes rose not quite high enough to meet the wolf's gaze, but the wide smile populated by rather sharp teeth below them. The grin widened in anticipation. "Yes, er. They ... they look quite nice. I'll have a pair."

"I got two pair."

"Yes, both thank you, sir."

"Now for you." The warewolf turned to the Disorganizationist.

The man listened while the warewolf went into his spiel, knowing beyond a doubt that he would agree to buy anything those teeth recommended.

Okradude kicked several dwarves out of its way and plucked one from the battling force. It lifted the unfortunate warrior high into the air as it plucked an okra lock from the back of its head. The dwarf squirmed and thrashed but couldn't get loose from the demon's two-fingered grip.

It squeezed the dwarf until he opened his mouth to gasp for air.

"No ye don't!" Durgen sprinted toward Okradude and leapt—not high at all—into the air. He drew his mallet back and brought it down on Okradude's foot with all the force a dwarf's arms could generate. Which was a lot.

Quite a lot.

Time was having the, ahem, time of its life. As Durgen Splurgenragher's mallet transformed many of the bones in Okradude's foot to porridge, Time thought it best to allow the demon to truly appreciate the sensation.

Having been largely forgotten once the fighters of FWMS had arrived, Bloomara had little trouble finding the others. "We must find the nymph and stop her before she has a chance to truly irritate Queen Mab."

"Why?" Fecanya asked. "Let her go over there and get slapped around a little. Got nothing to do with us. It's not even in this dimension."

Bloomara shook her head so hard the blue curls on her head jiggled. "You don't understand. Queen Mab will be irritated by all of this!"

Fecanya blinked. "Where's the part where I care?"

Garbita made a strangled sound and turned to Fecanya. "Queen *Mab* likes to take her *frustrations* out on just about every*one* else, any*where* else."

Fecanya opened her mouth to respond when her mind brought her up to speed. She imagined tornadoes having their way with giant mounds of abandoned powdered manure in processing plants. Hurricanes flung bovine frisbees through the sky.

She swallowed. All knew the power of Queen Mab, as well as her indiscriminate joy at making others miserable.

"I think I just spotted her," Mewamina said. She pointed at the edge of town where a grinning Siraka watched the chaos. She clapped her hands, her eyes alight with excitement. When she noticed the fairies watching her, she blew them a kiss, then used her wand to open a portal. With a sizable force in tow, she stepped through.

"Get after her," Mewamina said. She flew to the front of the group and gave bow at the waist. "I'll help out, here."

"You're not coming with us?" Fecanya asked.

Mewamina shook her head. "I may be able to communicate and—mostly—cooperate with felines, but I know them. If they set foot in Fey they'll instantly side with Queen Mab long before we'd reach our goal. We'd all end up as gifts on the front porch of her palace. I'm more useful in this world. Trust me."

"All right, then. Let's move!" Bloomara drew her wand and magicked a portal behind them. "We've no time to waste."

Twenty-Eight

Rolling blue-green fields and florescent flora greeted the fairies upon their arrival into Fey. Veins of running streams stretched into the distance, the clear white water dancing over the smooth colorful rocks below.

Four-winged birds with long, sharp beaks, and razor talons flew overhead in a W formation—because the V formation has been done to death —their feathers glowing with otherworldly brilliance.

They flew into a patch of trees that grew in shapes that would give earth trees a horrible bit of the scoliosis, and settled down near the top.

As one, they looked to the north.

"It's been a very long time since I've been here," Tootheria said, a nervous edge to her voice. "Still feels the same, though."

Fecanya nodded. "Yup. Almost feels like you can get drunk on magic in this place."

"Because we've spent so many ages in the earth realm," Bloomara stated.

The others nodded absently.

Fecanya noticed everyone staring in the same direction. No doubt they felt the power of Mab's Queendom radiating from the north, just as they felt the power of Titania's Queendom from the south.

"I've forgotten what it's like here," Caffeinisa said. She rubbed her temples. "It feels like being squeezed in a vice between those two. I don't know how anyone not aligned with either side can bear it."

"Just like anything else," Fecanya said, gathering herself to take off. "You get used to it. And I don't want to, so let's get moving before ..."

Garbita grabbed her by the shoulder and pulled her down.

"Oomph." She glared up at Garbita, but then followed her nervous gaze to the sky.

A pink dragon glided lazily overhead. Occasionally it flapped its great, leathery wings, pink puffs wafting from its nostrils. Sunlight bounced off of its shimmering scales and split into dozens of strands, scattering in every direction.

The fairies remained crouched low in the branches until the great beast was little more than a dot on the horizon. They slowly rose and flew into the sky.

"That was a close one." Fecanya nodded to Garbita. "Thanks, if that thing had spotted us—"

POOF.

Midsentence, Fecanya heard the ominous sound and she went silent. At the sight of her horror-stricken companions, she slowly turned to see the distant pink cloud that had been the dot that had been the dragon.

When she turned back, the other fairies' faces had added a pinch of ashen resolve to horror-stricken.

The great dragon lowered its huge head until its vertical slitted eye was right in front of the fairies. A low, deep rumble drifted from its parted jaws that made the fairies' teeth chatter.

It was all Fecanya could do to keep her body from shaking uncontrollably. She pointed past her companions. "Um ... I ... um."

Six trembling bodies rotated to face the dragon's humongous eye.

"Hello there, Mr. Dragon." Sugressa waved a trembling hand.

The dragon puffed another pink cloud from its nostrils and snatched the fairies out of the air with one massive claw.

For a time, all they could do was sit in terrified darkness. Fecanya heard the whoosh of wind with every flap of the dragon's great wings. *Knew I shouldn't have come to this blasted place. Humans may bumble all the time but at least they're largely oblivious. Now I'm about to be a snack.*

"What's going to happen to us?" Sugressa asked from somewhere in the darkness.

"It's taking us to its nest where it'll confess the great difficulties of being a pink dragon," Caffeinisa answered. "What do you think is going to happen? We're either going to be bite-sized hors d'oeuvres for this thing, or for its offspring."

Silence stretched in the darkness before Sugressa responded. "That sounds terrible."

"Just be ready to make a break for it when it opens its claw," Bloomara said. "Scatter in different directions to confuse it."

"You really think that'll work?" Tootheria said.

"Better than nothing," Fecanya replied.

The claw rocked and they heard the quaking sound of the dragon touching down.

"Get ready," Bloomara said.

The claw opened, just enough to show the huge, slitted eye looking in on them. "I really gotta thank you all for showing up."

"I've not had company in ages," the dragon said. "Good 'n all that, that I have excellent ears 'n all that to hear your wings. Also good that I got good eyes 'n all that. Otherwise I wouldn't have seen you all rising out of the tree to wave me down."

Fecanya realized her mouth was hanging open and shut it. "Er ... we, we weren't—"

"I haven't many friends 'n all that, you know? Used to be lots living around this region, but just as I got in and settled all comfy, you see, something happened and they all disappeared, they did. It's like a plague came in the night and took 'em 'n all that.

"I ever tell you about the dragonlands? Great place, and huge 'n all that. Like full of the magic. But then one day a bunch of folks up and disappeared. It was like something swept in on the night and then they were gone, by the way did you ever hear of a place southeast of here, just beyond the mango mountains. Best place for ..."

"We're going to die right here," Vegetina whispered while the dragon burbled on. "A looooong time from now, but trust me, we're done."

"... ham sandwich, like from what I hear about the human world, but I've never seen one. I used to have an ogre friend tell me all about 'em, but then one night I was asleep, I woke and then he was gone. Like one night a cloud came through and swept him on with it and he was gone, you see."

"You ever heard of Melvin the Verbose?" Vegetina whispered from the side of her mouth."

Fecanya felt her wings shrivel. "You mean the dragon who only stops talking long enough to sleep?"

Vegetina gave a barely perceptible nod. "If we don't get away from him, we'll be here for probably as close to eternity as you can get. Anyone who's gotten away did so during his naps, but usually he just closes his claw around you. His escaped victims had more luck than anything else."

"... nasty bit of the green wing, you see. It's a fungus you get when you ..."

"I welcome any suggestions," Fecanya said. "Maybe even self-impalement."

"... have any idea how hard it is, being a pink dragon? All the stereotypes ..."

"Mr. Dragon?" Sugressa thrust her hand into the air and waved it side to side. "Mr. ... Melvin, it is?"

"... pie crust that was just *dandy* and, hmm?" Melvin turned his attention to Sugressa. "You say something? I mean, I was getting to the good part, you see."

"Apologies for interrupting, Mr. Melvin the Verbose," Sugressa continued before the dragon could get going again. "It's just that we're kind of in a hurry. You see, we have to get going to the north as quickly as possible. It's really important."

"Oh." The dragon's crestfallen tone settled over the group like a pall.

Fecanya felt more guilt in that moment than she'd felt in her entire existence. She looked to the others and saw the same sentiment in every face. Even the haughty Bloomara's wings drooped.

"Blast it all," Vegetina growled. "He's using his magic on us. We've got to get away while we still *want* to get away andIfeellikecrying." Vegetina's shoulders bounced as she broke into sobs.

"No, you don't understand, Sugressa said, barely phased by Melvin's guilt magic. "It's not that we're not interested, but we've come here in pursuit of a friend and ... and all that."

"Oh. Really?" Melvin opened his claw some more and the guilt magic lifted, just a bit.

The fairies gathered themselves to bolt. Sugressa kept her arms at her sides, but she frantically waved her hands at them.

Everyone froze, eyeing each other but not daring to move.

"We're heading to the far north, Mr. Melvin," Sugressa continued. "Our friend is there."

Melvin scratched his scaly head with a rather sharp talon. It kicked up sparks. "Seems an odd place to go willingly, I have to say."

Sugressa flew up to the dragon and whispered something in his ear.

The grin that spread on Melvin the Verbose's face would have painted a yellow fear-stripe down the back of a saber-toothed tiger. "Heheh. Now I getcha. Well alrighty then. Good luck unscrambling your friend. Just say my name when you're ready and I'm there to help. See ya!"

POOF.

Pink cloud.

TWENTY-NINE

"I still can't believe you got Melvin to let us go," Vegetina said. "I've never heard of such a thing."

They sped across fields, meadows, and forests glowing in every color of the spectrum. A golden haze drifted lazily across the pastel-colored landscape, orange and blue, green and yellow rippling meadows passing below.

"Sometimes you just have to know how to negotiate." Sugressa winked.

Fecanya's confused frown deepened. "I've been wracking my brain on this, but I can't come up with an answer. How were you not affected by his guilt magic?"

Sugressa tapped a finger to her lips. "Well, that would probably be my nature! There's just too much to be happy and excited about to let some ole drab magic drag you down, you know?"

The other fairies nodded dubiously.

Fecanya smirked. "Translation; Cloy, here, is always flying so high that Melvin's magic probably only dragged her down to just above normal for anyone else."

Lines creased Sugressa's forehead. "I'm not that bad, am I? You really think I'm so overly cheerful as to be so sickening, Fecanya?"

Oh, great. Guilty without any guilt magic. "Of course not. It's just my little nickname as a term of endearment. Kinda like how Davin Gravelchin calls that goblin, Jackson, 'skinny neck'."

"Davin also threatens to wring Jackson's neck at least once a day," Sugressa added.

Fecanya became aware of everyone watching her. "Okay look." She felt heat rising up her face. "Look I don't mean it to be mean, okay? It's just a nickname. Like ..." she waved her hands emphatically. "Like you're just so sweet and cheerful I can hardly stand it. Kinda like when a human says something tastes so good they can hardly stand it, but they want more. You know?"

A big smile spread across Sugressa's face. "Really?"

To her own personal nausea, Fecanya smiled back. "Really."

Sugressa zipped a circle around Fecanya and wrapped her in a crushing hug. "Thank you!"

"Oomf! C'mon now! Knock it off. We're trying to ... we're trying to do something serious, here." She flapped her hand northward. "Can't have that nymph and Queen Mab see us being all mushy. It's a respect thing."

They formed magical barriers around themselves to resist the high-altitude winds, and rose high into the sky.

"Oooooh look!" Sugressa pointed out two large—even from their altitude—winged animals hunched over something in a clearing below. "It's a pair of gryphons grazing in that field!"

Fecanya shared a look with Garbita and Vegetina; the latter put her fist to her mouth and cleared their throat.

"She serious?" Caffeinisa whispered from the side of her mouth to Bloomara, who nodded.

"Just ... don't say anything. She's rather, er, sensitive about these sorts of things."

Caffeinisa frowned at the beaming Sugressa. "How many centuries before the naïveté starts to wane?"

"She's a sugar fairy," was all Tootheria said in answer. "I once had to fight one before I was finally able to convince her that there was very much such a thing as too much sweets, regardless of how much children affirmed the opposite. They're a ... special type, sugar fairies."

"I think I've spotted our dryad." Caffeinisa pointed out a lone figure in the distance surrounded by what must have been dozens of imps.

The fairies descended, but kept their distance above and behind the traveling creatures. Ahead, beyond a league of snow mounds and sparkling blue and green trees stood a castle of ice.

Fecanya held a forearm in front of her face. The amount of magic rippling from Mab's queendom even from this distance reminded her of the time she sat invisibly on a counter behind a baker just as she'd opened the oven and the blast of hot air nearly knocked her over.

"Mph." Caffeinisa turned her head away. "How can she stand it."

"You'll adjust," Tootheria replied. "Hits you a little harder, the longer you've been away."

Fecanya forced herself to pull her arm away and opened herself to it. She closed her eyes and spread her arms. Pure, raw fey magic swirled around her, through her. It filled her being and she rode the intoxicating wave, filled to the brim with the very stuff that made her and every citizen of Fey what they were.

The clearing of a throat penetrated her revel. She cracked an eye open to see her companions staring at her. Garbita looked away, her chin trembling above a wrinkled grin. Caffeinisa ran a hand over her mouth to hide her smile.

"It ... really does feel awesome," Sugressa tried. "All this magic and, and pure ... magic, and energy, you know?"

"Ahem, I think we should make our move soon," Bloomara said.

Fecanya raised her eyebrows, hardly expecting to be spared an awkward moment by her, of all fairies. "Yeah. Maybe we can stop this before it gets ..." she trailed off when a dozen snow trolls suddenly climbed out of the mounds to the left of Siraka's little band. Another group of trolls clambered out of snow mounds on the other side and behind the force.

"Yup. This is pretty bad," Fecanya said.

"But, snow trolls are *residents* of Queen Mab's *queen*dom," Garbita said. "Why would they *turn* ag*ainst* her?"

"Look closer," Vegetina said, and they did.

Fecanya squinted across the distance at the trolls for several moments, and then she saw it.

A troll at the front of the group on the left yanked at the pink and green barrettes adorning its braided white head, affording Fecanya a view of the purple-dyed fur under its arms. Its breath puffed between its tusks with each angry stomp of its feet. The orange and yellow legwarmers on its legs somehow repelled the snow and remained bright and pristine ... and visible for miles.

A snow troll on Siraka's other side tore at the black and white tuxedo it wore, but the suit remained undamaged and on its person.

"Welp," Fecanya said. "I don't think Siraka's going to have a problem finding allies."

"That's so cruel," Sugressa said. She pointed at a troll laboring to keep up with its comrades. "Trolls aren't meant to wear big beanies and skinny jeans."

"What about a pink bonnet and yellow-painted toenails?" Tootheria remarked.

"I'm pretty sure those aren't painted," Fecanya replied.

Garbita held her hand over her mouth. "Oh that is just ghastly!"

"We must intercept them before her ranks swell any further," Bloomara said, while Siraka's ranks continued with a good bit of swelling. "Come!" She drew her wand, pointed it at the force below, and bellowed incoherently."

The fairies watched in amusement as Bloomara and Garbita—wands leading—descended on Siraka and her growing army.

"Guess we'd better back them up," Tootheria said.

Vegetina arched an eyebrow. "Oh?" She jabbed a thumb at the speeding fairies below. "Don't let that bloom fairy get your arse kicked."

Tootheria conceded the point with a shrug. "However, if we stay here and they get pummeled, you think they'll just leave us be?"

"They will if we're in Tahiti," Caffeinisa said.

Tahiti sounds nice, Fecanya thought, envisioning frozen fruity drinks and adding to her little colored umbrella collection. She had just gotten the latest installment of The Adventures of Super Lady Marmalade and had been looking for an excuse to crack it open. *My new book and a nice, frozen margarita would be great right about now.*

"We can't let them fight by themselves." Sugressa drew her wand and flew after the others. "C'mon, Fecanya!"

The others drew their wands and looked at Fecanya, and she glowered at them. *Sugar broad didn't even bother to look back. Like she just* knew *I'd come.* She went.

Bloomara and Garbita reached them first. They hovered a dozen feet away in front of Siraka, wands pointed at her face.

"Don't even *think* about taking another step." Bloomara declared.

Siraka chuckled. "Whatcha gonna do, flower sprite? Bloom me to death?"

"That's a lot of lip from someone named after a sauce," Fecanya said. She and the rest of the fairies surrounded them, hovering well out of reach.

"My name is Sir*aka*, not Sriracha, you horse's arse!"

"Sounds like it'd be good on tacos," Fecanya replied.

The nymph cursed through her clenched teeth, but then shook her head and smiled. "You know, I had a feeling you and your little saucy mouth—"

"Because you know tons about sauce ..."

Siraka's nostrils flared. "I knew you'd find me here, so I asked a friend to keep you company."

A feeling of enclosure subtly crept up on her, and Fecanya's eyes widened. "Get back!" she yelled at the others as she turned and sped away. She hit an invisible substance that stretched as she pushed against it. Once her strength played out, the substance rebounded like a rubber band and threw her like an arrow straight into the snow.

Six thuds and grunts later told her that the others had met a similar fate. She climbed out of her snow hole and looked up—way up—at the troll standing over her.

From its penny loafer—complete with a penny in each pocket—shod feet, to orange and electric blue jogging suit and matching bowler, the troll would have towered over a tall human.

A shiver ran down Fecanya's spine. "No. Nononon00000."

The troll crouched over her and lowered its face until it was inches in front of her. Even the frowns creasing its forehead were bigger than Fecanya's whole body.

It looked her over with wide, black eyes, and its crusty lips peeled back into an open-mouthed smile.

"Hey there, little lady," the troll rumbled. Its forehead wrinkled some more when it looked up at the bowler on its head. "I'd take off me hat in courtesy if I could, but we can't take nothing of this ridiculous garb off, you see."

Fecanya opened her mouth to speak.

The troll said "heh," at the exact same time.

Rotten meat, cheese, and spiced haggis in cloud form drifted swiftly into her mouth.

Luckily, Fecanya was able to think faster than her reflexes, for if she'd closed her mouth, she would have trapped and swallowed the odors and they would have remained with her forever.

Her mouth still hanging open, she held up a finger to forestall the troll, used her other finger to wipe the tears from her eyes, and turned away and waited for the odor to grow bored and drift away. Snow melted in its wake.

Fecanya turned back, scooped some remaining snow into her still open mouth—she dared not close it yet—and swished it around.

The troll waited patiently, then said, "Our friend Ceramic, here, says that you fairies are from the world with all the talking primates. Says you like trivia."

Despite the retained smugness of her smile, Siraka balled her hands into fists.

"Says you like a good game of trivia, you do."

Fecanya froze. The others were just climbing out of their own snow holes and had no idea what was about to befall them.

"... but I'm forgetting me manners," the troll went on. "Name's Fonzerrelli, but you can call me Fonzerrelli. And noooooow ..." he hopped back and pounded his fists on his chest. "It's time for *Fiiiiiiiive Questiooooooons!*"

Gameshow music blared from no particular direction.

For what must have been the dozenth time in the span of a day, Fecanya's mouth fell open.

The other fairies's gaped at him.

"We're gonna have some fun, ladies!" Fonzerrelli went on. "What's gonna happen is you're gonna stay here with me while Ms. Ceramic ..."

"Si ... ra ... ka," Siraka growled.

"... takes the rest of the folks there up to Queen Mab's castle to pick a fight."

"I'm not *picking* a *fight*, you mildewy—"

"... get started, shall we?"

"Ooooh I *love* games!" Sugressa hopped up and down and sank back into the snow. Her hand popped out of the hole with a muffled "can I go first?"

Vegetina managed to sidle up beside Fecanya. "I've heard of this guy;

Fonzerrelli the Trivia Troll. If we don't answer all five of his questions correctly, he'll start with five new ones, and they get harder each time. He won't let us go until we've answered five in a row correctly."

"And that funky forest girl magicked a dome over us so we can't get away," Fecanya replied. "I *swear*, when I get a hand on her I'm going to shave her bald and magic it permanently to her chin!"

"One thing at a time," Vegetina said as Sugressa flew up to hover in front of the troll.

Siraka watched the sugar fairy conversing with the Trivia Troll and the corner of her mouth twitched. She shook her head. "Have fun, sprites."

With a wave of her hand, Siraka and the rest of her troll force departed.

Fecanya scowled at the nymph's back. *I am going to* ... a giant, bratwurst-sized finger tapped her on the shoulder, sending her sprawling into the snow.

"*Oops,*" she heard a muffled voice say from outside of the snow in her ears. A hand lifted her out and deposited her in the middle of the semi-circle of her companions.

"All right, then." Fonzerrelli rubbed his hands together.

Fecanya tried not to think about the origin of whatever crusty substance it was that fell away. *I'm going to get very creative when I get my hands on that nymph...* her eyes widened as an idea dawned on her. She looked back to Fonzerrelli. "Hey, I think you'd like ..."

Fonzerrelli stopped her with an upheld finger. "First off. *Who* was the first troll to suffer from Top Head Baldness?"

THIRTY

The landscape was little more than a blur, far below, as the fairies sped across the sky. Fecanya basked in the frigid air blowing across her face. It was going to be a good day.

"You're quite pleased with yourself," Vegetina remarked.

Fecanya winked. "This is going to be good, trust me."

"We had to go *six rounds* with that lummox before he would even *listen* to you," Garbita complained. "Siraka is likely *assaulting* Mab's *castle* by now."

"That reminds me of a question," Tootheria said. "Why are we trying to stop her, anyway. If she wins the fight ..."

Caffeinisa snorted.

"... she'll probably take over the castle, or something. Not like it'll affect us in the earth realm. If she loses the fight, she's still out of our hair." Tootheria shrugged. "Win, win."

"Not exactly," Fecanya said. "Even if wood woman pulled a miracle and beat Mab, she doesn't have the magic to sustain winter in Fey."

"And she *certainly* doesn't have the *power* to prevent the absolute *drubbing* Queen Mab's sister or any of the other powerful sidhe would *inflict* on her."

Tootheria shrugged again. "I still don't see how that affects us."

"She's not going to defeat Queen Mab," Bloomara said. "Even if they were to fight in the summer queendom of Titania's domain, where Mab's power is at its least, Siraka would have no chance of matching her, let alone in the winter queendom where her power is at its height. And to your point," she added just as Tootheria started to shrug again. "Queen Mab has a habit of continuing on, once she gets going."

"After having whatever fun she has with Siraka and her army," Fecanya added. "She'll decide that since the dryad is from the earth realm, she'll go there to continue the fun."

Bloomara nodded. "It'll start with her mermaid friends tricking drunken sailors to get fresh with lobsters. Then the next thing you know, she's whispering to the chimpanzee population that humans are making fun of them. You ..." she rapidly shook her head. "You don't want to see that, trust me."

The air grew ever colder and the snow thicker. Ice-born structures sparkled in the cold sun, while their inhabitants looked up at the passing fairies with "you poor bastards" expressions. The sounds and smell of magic and explosions signaled that the battle had already begun. Tiny dots below darted in every direction, sending green gouts of magic up and down the streets. Boulders arced across the sky to be blasted apart by sidhe warriors.

"Welp, looks like we're late," Vegetina said.

Fecanya clapped her hands together. "Welp, indeed. It was a good run, girls. Guess we might as well head back."

"Do you not remember a thing I said, earlier? Bloomara asked. "The aftermath of this battle will follow us into the human world."

"Humans are resilient. They'll be fine."

"They'll tear the world apart trying to battle Mab," Bloomara replied. "And Mab will simply leave when she's had her fill."

Fecanya responded with a wrinkled upside-down smile, shrugged, and held out her hands. "We could actually do the same."

Sugressa turned an incredulous expression on her. "You don't mean that, Fecanya!"

Fecanya stuck out her hand. "Allow me to introduce myself. I'm a shit fairy. How about you?"

A stray magic bolt whizzed through the middle of the hovering fairies and they flinched away.

Garbita swore a litany of creative expletives. drew her wand and flew straight into the battle.

They watched the Detritus Redistributor sock a troll square in the eye, then blast an advancing sidhe warrior in the mouth with a gust of what must have been *essaunce de garbauge*, judging by the way his back buckled as he turned aside to purge.

Magic and projectiles—some organic, some not—sped back and forth between the battling forces. Surprisingly, Siraka's army was pushing the sidhe forces back, inch by inch toward Mab's castle. Angry, terribly dressed trolls hurled trees, boulders, and even each other at the defenders.

Grinning imps—those who weren't snatched out of the air by a troll with nothing to throw—hurled spears and black magic at the winter forces. The tiny devils stung the sidhe and retreated, their clumsy flight making them difficult targets for the larger, human-sized sidhe army.

Siraka spread her arms wide, and tree roots bulged from the ground. They tore through stone streets and burst out of ice buildings and smashed into the side of a sidhe contingent.

The nymph drew her wand and flicked it in the direction of a sidhe captain barking commands. His words suddenly came out as cat mewling.

She flicked her wand at another warrior and he dropped to his knees, holding his mouth as an extra row of teeth grew in.

Fecanya ducked a speeding projectile whose uncertain origin she didn't want to ponder. She waved her hands and thrust them out. Her shield appeared just in time to stop the splatter of whatever it was a snow troll had thrown at her.

Tootheria aimed her wand at an advancing troll and let fly a barrage of magical teeth. The enamel missiles punched the beast in the eyes and somehow slipped past its bow tie to strike it in the throat. When it opened its maw in a silent gasp, Fecanya filled it with a magical cloud of eu de ordure. The troll's eyes widened. It turned away and spewed all over a nearby sidhe warrior battling a cluster of imps.

Imp laughter echoed down the street until a sidhe warrior threw a net over them and hurled them into the face of nearby troll. They went down in a tangle of leathery wings and wrinkled hockey jersey.

The air grew suddenly colder. Fecanya felt a shiver that had nothing to do with the cold, and looked toward the castle.

Queen Mab stood at the top of the many stairs leading up to her castle

—well, she stood upon a raised platform held aloft by four ogres so everyone could see her—and looked down upon the battle. The ogres—there were four of them, just for effect, as a rodent could have carried the fairy queen on its back—descended the steps, the grinning Mab looking over the chaos with wide-eyed glee.

The arrival of the winter queen halted the battle as though both forces had frozen where they stood. The sidhe forces turned and parted before the grinning Mab.

"There you are, you portabella-sized rat." Siraka sashayed through her army and stopped at its head.

"Such hostility," Mab replied, her voice cold and crystalline. "Do I know you?"

"I ... you ..." Siraka's mouth bobbed open and closed several times. She stabbed her finger toward the queen. "You know who I am! You set that stinking sailor on me. Had him bouncing me on his knee and everything before I punched him out. Do you have any idea the humiliation—"

Queen Mab laughed. "Oh, I remember, now. That was eighty-seven years ago, was it not?"

"Eighty-eight," Siraka muttered. "And I was still talking, thank you very much—"

"You're welcome." She flicked her fingers. "Your little show has entertained me, though you needn't have gone to such trouble to thank me for facilitating your little escapade on the docks, that night. I assure you the amusement was all mine."

Siraka's green hair stood on end and turned to wood. Her eyes blazed with anger, and the surrounding tree roots rose up and advanced on the winter queen. "I'll crush you—"

With a lazy wave of her hand, Mab stopped the roots and sent them burrowing back into the ground. She looked over Siraka's army and tilted her head. "What's this? Why have the trolls of my domain come bearing hostility?"

Hundreds of tusks bounced up and down as maws struggled to find words to respond. A few half-hearted mumbles about damp fur under otherwise comfortable sweatpants broke the silence, along with the occasional murmur about wanting to have white fur again instead of orange and fuchsia.

"Actually kinda *like* wearin' flip-flops," one snow troll said. He pointed at Siraka while still staring at his feet. "Forest girl tell me not to like it."

"I gots a fine thing with wearin' yellow sweaters," another troll said, pointedly ignoring the perspiration soaking through the garment. It also pointed a muscly finger at Siraka. "Cerebellum told me to come here for some reason to complain about it, but I likes the thing, I do."

Siraka stared in indignation at no one in particular, as finger after finger pointed at her.

Having carefully glided well back from the fight and hunkered inconspicuously in the underhang of roof, the fairies shared a look.

"That's cold," Vegetina whispered. "Her entire army just sold her out. Just like that."

Caffeinisa snorted.

Mab looked across several hundred yards, directly at them.

Fecanya sighed as they found themselves now standing between the queen and the nymph.

"Good going," Tootheria muttered at the caffeine fairy.

"This is unexpected," Mab said. She snapped her fingers, and the ogres knelt and placed her palanquin on the ground.

"Pray tell me, to what do I owe the pleasure of such visitors. I've not known Deliah to have such interest in my domain as to send a band of her employees here. Have you come to bear witness to ..." her gaze flickered over the seething Siraka, "the dryad's demise? I can assure you that what is about to happen to her will reverberate across all of Fey, and no doubt into the earth realm as well."

The winter queen's smile was like a frozen breeze piercing a tundra blizzard. "Perhaps it's been too long since last I visited up on the earth realm. Surely so. How else could a simple dryad grow enough impudence to enter my domain with rodent devils at her back?"

Several nearby imps stiffened

"Hey!" a rather foolish imp squeaked, then looked around as everyone discretely distanced themselves.

Queen Mab snapped her fingers. The imp found itself suddenly dressed in a red and brown striped polyester dinner jacket with matching slacks, and a dark brown cummerbund. The wide-eyed imp thrashed at the suit, but its little claws did nothing to damage the garment.

Mab turned back to the fairies.

"I assure you, Queen Mab," Bloomara began, wiping away perspiration from her brow. "We most certainly are not here to interfere with your affairs. We've come to—"

The winter queen waved her away. "It hardly matters. After I'm done with my ... guest, here, I will come to the earth realm. It's been too long, and I've grown bored."

Despite her show of courage, Siraka shivered. Sweat trickled down the side of her face. Her eyes darted left and right, for she now stood alone in the center of a growing circle comprised of Mab's forces as well as her own. She lifted her chin. It trembled.

"But then you'll miss out on the fun!" Sugressa exclaimed.

Queen Mab arched an eyebrow. "Really? And how so, sugar fairy?"

"It was *supposed* to be a surprise." Fecanya feigned a glare at Siraka that wasn't feigned. "But she had to go and ruin it by attacking you. We wanted to create a lovely show that would entertain you for very long time, Queen Mab."

Sugressa nodded emphatically. "We planned this out to be a really nice surprise, but now it's—"

"Yes, yes. Now it's ruined. Cease with your prattling and reveal it, child."

Sugressa and Fecanya flew straight into the air, put their fingers to their lips, and whistled.

Poof.

Pink cloud.

"Oh, woah! Hey there, Mab!"

Queen Mab's eyes widened, and she turned her frosty glare on Fecanya and Sugressa. "You've brought Melvin the Verbose into my queendom—"

A troll dressed in penny loafers, orange and electric blue jogging suit, and matching bowler hopped off of Melvin's back and bowed.

"I'd tip my hat, Ms. Queen," Fonzerrelli said. "But I can'ts take it off, you see, on account of your magic thing won't let me." He noticed Siraka and his eyes lit up. "Oh!" He waved. "Hey there, Serotonin!"

Sparks flew from Siraka's grinding teeth.

Queen Mab's left eye twitched.

"Better hurry up with that explanation," Vegetina whispered from the corner of her mouth.

"You see," Fecanya hurried on. "Every court should have entertainment. What better entertainment is there than Melvin the Verbose, Fonz-errelli the Trivia Troll, and Siraka the ... Forest Nymph," she cast Siraka an artificial apologetic look, "engaged in a nice game of trivia and stories?"

"WHAT?" Siraka whirled. "You little turd-tossing ..." curled fingers leading, Siraka threw herself at Fecanya.

Queen Mab never took her eyes off Fecanya and Sugressa. She snapped her fingers and the nymph stopped midair. "You have my interest."

"We imagined you haven't had a good show in a long time, and," Sugressa cleared her throat. "Melvin and Fonzerrelli definitely have the ... er ... stamina—"

A tiny smile found its way to the fairy queen's thin blue lips. "An endless show of trivia and stories for my little dryad, here." She clapped her hands together. "Excellent. Good work. I am pleased. This will surely provide many days of entertainment." She turned a devious grin on the suspended Siraka, who never took her desperately livid gaze off Fecanya and Sugressa. "*Many* days indeed."

THIRTY-ONE

"I must admit," Bloomara said to Fecanya and Sugressa as they stepped through the portal back to the earth realm. "That was a brilliant idea."

"I know you're ornery to say the least, Vegetina said to Fecanya. But you," she grinned at Sugressa, "you've got a mean streak in you, sugar girl."

Fecanya thought about the last thing they'd seen before leaving. Mab had dressed Siraka in an evening gown complete with puffy shoulder pads, and her hair styled in a manner befitting a 90s mullet rock band.

She'd created an entire new wing of her castle as an audience chamber for all to enjoy the show. Fonzerrelli had been given a stage with moving lights and the whole shebang, while Melvin had already hunkered down to start talking even as everything was being constructed around them.

Despite the sweet taste of revenge, Fecanya shuddered.

"Why do you say that?" Sugressa asked.

"Well," Vegetina said. "It was bad enough that Fecanya got Siraka condemned to an eternity of playing Five Questions with the Trivia Troll, but at least she gets to interact with him. *You* added in the endless one-sided conversation with Melvin the Verbose. Far worse, in my opinion. Remind me not to get on your bad side."

"It's not like that," Sugressa said. "It wasn't to hurt Siraka—"

"Speak for yourself," Fecanya said.

"But to save her from Mab."

Caffeinisa snorted. "Save her?"

Sugressa nodded. "Queen Mab has a way of getting revenge that can be very uncomfortable and last a *long* time. Siraka is a dryad. Queen Mab would have done something to make her permanently uncomfortable, like making her live near fire, or crafting an ice structure in the shape of a tree and forcing her to live in it forever."

"That's a weird sort of torture," Bloomara replied.

Vegetina nodded her understanding. "Not for a forest nymph. They don't like fire, for obvious reasons, and the cold makes all but those tied to evergreens go dormant. And since Siraka's tree isn't in this world, living in a structure fashioned like a tree and made of ice ..." she sighed.

"Just sitting in there, on ice made to look like your home but isn't. And you're cold, forever." A rare frown creased Sugressa's brow. "I know Siraka is in for some not very happy days ahead—"

"More like centuries," Fecanya added.

"But at least she'll be more comfortable."

"Well, that is something," Tootheria said. "If she doesn't go insane." She gave Sugressa and Fecanya an approving nod. "That was some good negotiating, getting Mab to create a magical equivalent that's tied to Siraka's real tree."

"I guess we make a good team, sometimes, Cloy," Fecanya said. She gave Sugressa an awkward pat on the shoulder.

Sugressa beamed. "Thanks, Fecanya!"

They stepped out of the portal and into the final stages of a cleanup effort.

"Quite impressive," Garbita said. "They've nearly got the *town* back in one *piece* again. It looks like all of FWMS is here."

Indeed, many of the staff of Fey World Maintenance Services hummed about the aftermath of the battle. Brownies cleaned the streets while waiting for the dwarves to repair broken homes and businesses so they could go in and sweep.

Gnomes repaired lawns and gardens, replanted and revitalized the city flora, and tended the traumatized local animals.

On the sidelines, one fairy per several dozen humans kept the primates in a state of blissful ignorance. The crowds stood in glassy-eyed happiness, completely unaware of anything happening around them.

The goblins mostly stayed out of the way.

A muscular fairy with flaming yellow hair, hard, green eyes, and arms crossed above titanium hard abs oversaw the project with stern approval.

Fecanya froze. Deliah Harmass. She looked from the Lead Supervisor to Tootheria and back. As inconspicuously as she could manage, she receded from the front of the group to slip beside Tootheria. "Don't you think you deserve a vacation after this whole ordeal. I mean, you were kidnapped and all."

Tootheria thought on that for a moment and shook her head. "Nah. I really should get back—"

"Ssssshhhh. No need to talk so loud," Fecanya hissed. I'm right here."

Tootheria leaned away. "You're right, so why not get away from my ear, Fecanya—"

"Nononono ..." Fecanya closed her eyes. Her shoulders slumped and her head fell back just before she heard the inevitable ...

"Fecanya?" With laser-like precision, Deliah Harmass turned on her heel and looked directly at Fecanya. "You're back. All of you." She walked over to stand before them. "You all look like you've been through quite an ordeal." She looked—or rather, analyzed—them over. "Yes, definitely an ordeal."

"The situation in Fey has been concluded, Lead Supervisor," Bloomara reported. "The assault on Queen Mab has been quelled, and she has no designs on entering this world."

Deliah sighed with relief. It was a subtle, unfamiliar thing from her. "Very well-done. All of you."

"The *lion's* share of that credit goes to *Sugressa* and *Fecanya*," Garbita said, then muttered, "as much as I'm *loathe* to admit the *latter*." She cleared her throat. "With*out* them, it may well have been a *dreadful conclusion*."

Deliah's eyebrows rose at that. "I see. Well-done, Fecanya and Sugressa."

"Oh, well, it really was all of us." Sugressa grinned. "We all did it together!"

"Indeed," Deliah said. She tilted her head. "Fecanya, are you all right? Why are you standing so still? What are you staring at?"

Fecanya, who had been doing her best to be as unnoticeable as possible, sighed. "Oh, nothing. I just, nothing."

Deliah gave her a dubious frown, then addressed them all. "Don't concern yourself with the cleanup efforts. You've done a fine job of tracking down and stopping the dryad, and thus preventing the doubtless catastrophe that would have been ..." she cleared her throat. "An untimely visitor from Fey."

The lead supervisor turned on her heel and strode back toward the cleanup efforts, then stopped. "Enjoy a much-deserved rest before resuming your duties. You've earned it. Oh, and good to have you back safe, Caffeinisa, Vegetina, and Tootheria. Mewamina filled me in on what happened. You girls are lucky."

When it appeared Deliah was about to turn away once more, she stopped and looked past everyone, straight to Fecanya. "Thank you for filling in as tooth fairy during Tootheria's absence, Fecanya. You may resume your duties as Ordure Engineer immediately."

"Of course," Fecanya replied with as much sweetness as an annoyed cassowary. She turned away. "May as well get started."

"There's no need to start right now—" Deliah started to repeat, but Fecanya cut her off.

"S'fine. The peace and quiet is fine. I'll be out in the woods. Besides, all that *ordure* must be managed. Wouldn't want everything to start over-flowing—"

"Actually," Vegetina cut in. I think I pulled a muscle through this whole ordeal. I was hoping to take a little extra time to heal." She turned to Fecanya and winked. "I'd been wanting to ask if you could fill in for me but I never got the chance." She turned back to a suspicious Deliah and shrugged. "Once I'm better, I'll fill in for Fecanya. I'm sure we'd all be willing to help out, since she and Sugressa saved the day."

Deliah looked over the various reactions, ranging from stunned silence to tooth gnashing. "I suppose that is fair. As long as the tasks are done, I'm fine with it. If you'll excuse me."

While Fecanya's shocked brain processed what had just happened, Mewamina arrived. She touched down in the center of the group, hugging them each in turn and filling them in on what happened while they were gone.

"Believe it or not," Mewamina said, "the one who saved the day was Zachary Von Badass."

"That wiry knotter?" Garbita said. "What could *he* have done rather than *yell* everyone to death."

"Well," Mewamina said. "When he regained consciousness after being knocked out twice, the enemy didn't really bother with him anymore. Then he jumped up on a pile of rubble and pointed at Butterbean Flinger, screaming about *beastmoooooood*. He climbed on the roof of the Galaxy Doe coffee shop, hopped from rooftop to rooftop to get to the giant demon."

"I can't believe the idiot didn't get himself killed," Bloomara said.

"Close." Mewamina snickered behind her hand. "I don't know what he was planning to do, but a stray magic bolt hit the corner of a roof just as he got to it. It sent him flying straight into Butterbean Flinger's nose."

Bloomara turned her head away and waved her hands. "No! I don't want to hear any more—"

"The thing sneezed so hard, it blasted Von Badass into the back of Durian Dude's head, along with several hundred giant butter beans. Knocked it and Zachary out cold. Butterbean Flinger fell backwards, right into Okradude, and they crashed into a strip mall. The tide turned after that."

"And now, cleanup," Caffeinisa said.

"Cleanup," Mewamina agreed. "Through some miracle a contingent of FWMS fairies arrived in time to block human technology and prevent all of this showing up on their phones and televisions. After that they put the brain whammy on them and corralled them in a little temporary pocket dimension until the battle was won. Couldn't keep them there long, though. Too much universal reality stuff, you see."

Fecanya listened with only half an ear. She wanted to go. Specifically, she wanted to go home, grab her new volume of The Adventures of Super-lady Marmalade, and go someplace tropical. She wondered what her iguana friend Linda was doing right now. She really wanted a frozen margarita.

She nearly jumped when Sugressa's voice said next to her. "You know, we can pull the load until you get back, Fecanya. I'm sure you'd like one of those fancy drinks at the beach and all."

"What makes you say that?"

Sugressa smirked. "The only time I've seen you smile like that is when you were on vacation, or when you're thinking about that vacation."

Fecanya shrugged. "Eh. I'm not special. No more entitled to take a trip right now than any of you."

"Our jobs are a little more fun than yours," Sugressa said. "No offense. I think that entitles you to a little break from time to time. Well, you and Garbita, anyway."

An unbidden stray thought of being on vacation with Garbita shot through Fecanya's mind before she could stop it. She gave her head a shake.

"Anyway," Sugressa went on. "I just wanted you to know that enough of us agreed to share the tasks until you get back. We'll be fine since Deliah is granting us all a little break before we get back to work."

Fecanya thought about everything they'd been through over the past year and nearly got emotional before she got a handle on herself. "Look, I'm not saying I *want* you to, or anything, but if you've got nothing else to do and you wanna come with me—"

"Really, Fecanya?" Sugressa wrapped her in a hug.

"Oomph! Get off, you're wrinkling my dress." She started to smooth her dress and nearly cut her hand on the burlap material. "Anyway, yeah, so, yeah." She started mumbling. "I'm gonna go home and grab a book, so if you—"

"I'll meet you there!" Sugressa hugged Fecanya again, then took off before she could complain.

"Pretty good friend you've got there," Vegetina said.

"Mmyeahshe'sallright."

Vegetina chuckled. "Before I transferred here, I worked at a facility down south. I know being an ordure engineer in this region isn't ideal ..."

Fecanya blinked slowly.

"Okay, it sucks under any scenario," Vegetina amended. "But trust me, it's extremely humid in some of those places. The ordure engineers over there are, perpetually snarky."

"So you're saying I should be nicer because I could be processing crap in a moister environment?"

Vegetina scrunched her face. "Please don't use the word "moist" when connected to this subject matter. Actually, just don't use the word "moist, at all. And no, that's not what I mean. I'm just saying that those girls have a rough go at being friends with anyone who's not an ordure engineer.

"Despite that crotchety thing you've got going," she swirled her finger at Fecanya, "you're likable enough to have a loyal friend in Sugressa."

"She's just like that," Fecanya said.

"Right. And she tolerates you calling her Cloy." Vegetina shrugged.

"Look, if you ever want someone to hang out with, I might be around, or whatever. I'm pretty sure Caffeinisa and Tootheria feel the same."

Before Fecanya could respond, Vegetina waved and took flight.

Fecanya watched until the vegetable fairy was out of sight. How in Lilith's underworld had she managed to make friends?

"Ahem."

Fecanya turned to see Garbita looking at her. She readied a particularly spicy remark, but the detritus redistributor looked as though she was about to be sick. "That ... well, that was a *fine* job you and *Sugressa* did back there, Fecanya. I ... don't *think* I would have *enjoyed* the *litter* Queen Mab and her *minions* would have left me to clean up. No, I wouldn't have." She waved an irritable hand. "Oh just *take* your bloody *vacation*, Fecanya. You'll be a right *foul* fairy if you don't. Good day."

A similar interaction with Bloomara left a stupefied Fecanya standing in shock, blinking. *What just happened?*

Tootheria, Mewamina, and Caffeinisa came to thank her and said their goodbyes, and then Fecanya stood by herself while the staff of Fey World Maintenance Services magicked the human town back to its former self.

Fecanya slipped into her flip-flops and snapped her fingers. A pair of sharp-edged sunglasses appeared in front of her and she slipped them on top of her head. Another snap produced her floppy beach hat.

On her way out, she opened her extra dimensional duffel bag and dropped in The Adventures of Superlady Marmalade Vol: 3. As she was about to leave, a letter appeared on her desk.

"Probably work related," she thought aloud, and started to leave again. Then she muttered a curse and snatched it off the desk.

Dear Miss Fecanya,

I hope this finds you well and in an unusually noncantankerous mood. As your therapist, I am possessed of the authority and responsibility to see to your mental and emotional well-being and, in the instance of your particular ... flavor, MY mental and emotional well-being, as well. As such ...

Fecanya could practically hear him clear his throat before beginning the next sentence.

I have recommended to Lead Supervisor Deliah Harmass that your vacation be extended for a month, that you may return to your duties in the least hostile temperament possible. Enjoy your stay, Miss Fecanya. We will resume our appointments upon your return.

Absolutely sincerely despite what you think,

Leowitriss,

FWMS Therapist

Fecanya stared at the letter, doing her best to push down the lump in her throat. *Doggon therapist. Trying to trick me into liking him. Ain't gonna work.*

She left her pod, zipped across the beehive-like rotunda, and met Sugressa at the exit. Moments later, she and Sugressa—who probably figured she was Fecanya's best friend, but she absolutely was *not, doggon it* —lay in cushioned chaise lounges on a warm beach, frozen margaritas in hand.

Linda had brought friends, and so the two fairies simply lay in the sun, battling freeze-brain with every sip, surrounded by sunbathing iguanas.

"I'm probably glad you came along," Fecanya mumbled.

A huge smile flashed across Sugressa's face but she quickly—wisely— holstered it. "Wouldn't want you getting all inebriated again, would we?"

"Mmph." She took another sip.

Sugressa leaned over and looked in Fecanya's bag. "Are those spectacles?"

Fecanya closed the bag. "Kinda. They're spectacles that mold to the bridge of any nose. The local fey community here specializes in sunshades, spectacles, blah blah. Figured I'd ... switch 'em with Leo's."

"Oh how nice! He'll love them." Sugressa clasped her hands in front of her chest. "What a nice gesture!"

"That you'll never survive to see, if you tell him," Fecanya replied. "I ... yeah well I figured it'd be a fun joke on him, watching him be all comfortable with no more headaches in his stupid new glasses and never suspect they're different. Jokes on him. Loser. Haha, yeah."

She side-eyed Sugressa, who simply stared out at the ocean. "That's, er, really gonna show him, Fecanya."

Fecanya started to say several things, then settled on, "Yeah."

She took another sip.

Acknowledgments

A very special shot out to Michelle Corsillo. Your help in putting this book together has been a lifesaver. Thank you!

Special shot out to Arthur Carnevale for helping bring Cruzindream the Sloth to life.

Last but not least, a huge thank you to Cat Lee, Karen Pellet, and Flora Samuelson. No book is written alone, and this one is better for having your hands in it.

About the Author

About the Author

Ramón Terrell is an author and actor who instantly fell in love with fantasy the day he opened R. A. Salvatore's: The Crystal Shard. Years (and many devoured books) later he decided to put pen to paper for his first novel. After a bout with aching carpals, he decided to try the keyboard instead, and the words began to flow.

When not writing, or acting, he enjoys reading, video games, hiking, and long walks with his wife around Stanley Park in Vancouver BC.

Ramonterrell.com

Also by Ramón Terrell

CPSIA information can be obtained
at www.ICGtesting.com
Printed in the USA
BVHW090953060922
646306BV00011B/569

9 781777 896485